Snow Moon

A Time Travel Romance Novella

Abby Rice

Clairitage Press

Contents

Chapter 1

RACHEL

I blew out a frustrated breath, but the curl in my eyes refused to budge. Even the clock on the far wall of the kitchen was silently mocking me.

Twenty minutes before the guests were due to arrive. And my jerk of a boss waits 'til *now* to inform me that four extra place settings are suddenly required?!

I glared at his narrow shoulders as he stomped from the kitchen, Italian loafers clicking on the tile floor. A perfectly-tailored back, from the drape of his charcoal pin-striped jacket, to the crisply-starched white collar protruding the regulation distance up his neck, to the immaculately-coiffed silver hair above that.

Hair spray, I decided. The sixtyish man must use hair spray to keep every silvery thread aligned just so, never a hair out of place despite his annoying habit of bustling around shouting impossible last-minute orders to everyone in sight.

Naturally, tonight of all nights, the soup isn't quite ready. With the largest party of the season set to descend soon. And somehow I was supposed to miraculously rustle up four more place-settings *some*where and try to squeeze them into the already-overcrowded dining tables, finish the soup, slice the bread, which should be coming out of the oven in – I glanced up at the clock again – six more minutes. And pour the waters. Sure thing. Piece of cake.

I resisted the urge to throw a mocking military salute at Mr. Devon Williams' ramrod-straight back.

Patience, I urged myself. *Rent's due next week. I can't afford to lose this job.*

At least I enjoyed cooking. Or I would, if Dastardly Devon weren't in charge.

Catering was hardly what I'd imagined myself doing right now. But then, I hadn't imagined the auto accident last year on Tahoe's snowy roads that took both my parents. Hadn't imagined that, at age twenty-three, I'd suddenly find myself *in loco parentis* to a moody seventeen-year-old, my younger sister, Serena. Hard to believe, but only a year ago I'd been happily enrolled in pre-med courses at the local college, blithely anticipating a career as a doctor in the not-too-distant future.

Now, an impossibly-distant future.

A year ago, I was cooking up stuff in the chem labs. I never pictured myself standing over a commercial-size pot of brilliant-orange carrot soup in the kitchen of the historic Glenbrook House.

Sure, it's a cool old building. One of Tahoe's first waystations, built back in 1863. Perched half a mile from the lake and brilliantly restored within an inch of its life. A delight for tourists and locals alike, with charmingly renovated rooms and a spacious dining hall for catered events like this one. *A wedding reception, so everything must be perfect*, as Devon had already warned me four times, now.

If it wasn't for Serena, I wouldn't be putting up with Devon the Drill Sergeant. I'd be blissfully immersed in lectures on brain function and blood chemistry, or whipping up a bit of culinary magic for myself on weekends. Maybe even dating from time to time. Heaven knows I hadn't been on a real date in – I blew unsuccessfully at that errant lock of hair on my forehead again. I couldn't even remember. *Far too long.*

Not since the accident. Not since the judge's gavel smacked down, dubbing me Serena's official guardian. Not since I'd dropped out of college and moved us into a tiny apartment we could *kinda, sorta* afford. *As long as I keep this job.*

I gave the bright orange soup another frustrated stir, trying to recall where extra place-settings might be found.

Serena was worth every bit of it. My sparkling, funny, impossibly annoying sister. To be honest, I couldn't remember what *I* was like at seventeen, but surely I was never this grumpy. This opinionated. This moody.

The two of us had always been close. That helped. But now I was trying to play mom as well as older sister, and it wasn't working. As Serena found increasingly creative ways to let me know. We might be sisters, but in some ways we were polar opposites, too. Serena was lithe where I tended toward chunky. The Italian gene came through much louder in my jet-black hair and brown eyes. She was petite with green eyes setting off her waist-length brown hair, a touch of the Irish to soften the Sicilian heritage we shared. At five-foot-nine I still had three inches on her. But the way she'd shot up this past year I wouldn't be able to glare down at her much longer.

Our lives had fractured neatly into "BA" and "AA." *Before the accident. After the accident.* An A-student before our parents died, Serena was currently pulling a steady diet of Ds. Once a proud member of the chess club, the swim club, and the track team, she'd been forced to quit all three because we only had one car, and I needed it for work. Sure, we were scraping by financially. But in the things that truly counted, I was worried.

She found plenty of ways to entertain herself while I wasn't home, of course. None of them good. Her best friend? Arrested for shoplifting, as Serena casually informed me yesterday. "But they won't do anything to her; she's still a juvenile." Her shrug accompanied a faint, worldly grin.

And then there was Mark. The epicenter of our most recent blow-ups. "Cool and sophisticated" Mark who, according to the few details Serena let leak, seemed impressively adept at getting hold of alcohol and weed, and disturbingly unmotivated by school.

Though we fought almost continually these days, Serena still meant everything to me. And I tried to make sure she knew it. Her fleeting smile when I got home magically erased any tiredness from long catering shifts. Just knowing she was still in school somehow felt like a triumph.

Life wasn't perfect. But together, we were making it.

Mom and Dad would have done it so much better, of course. I missed them terribly. But now all I had left was my sister. And I was worried about losing her, too. To drugs. To the street. To her ill-chosen infatuation with Mark. I wasn't a great substitute parent. But I was doing my best.

I heard myself sigh and the fingers of my left hand reached automatically for the pendant I always wore around my neck. A gift from Mom for my birthday, two weeks before she died. The gem was some sort of blue-white crystal – she hadn't told me what, and I'd never bothered to take it to a jeweler to find out.

"Do what you love," Mom used to say. Well, I *was* doing that. I did love cooking. At least when Devon the Domineering wasn't barking last-minute orders. I'd also enjoyed school. I gave the pot of soup a determined stir, wondering if I'd ever see the inside of those pre-med classrooms again.

For the moment, anyway, college definitely wasn't part of the plan.

The rumble of thunder interrupted, drawing my eyes to the window. This was the first week of February, so a chill seeped through the walls like it always did at Lake Tahoe. But the newlyweds were in luck this evening; there'd been no snow for several weeks, and the temperature outside hovered slightly above freezing.

A giant full moon was already rising over the treetops – the Snow Moon, Serena had called it. She'd looked it up. The name an encouraging reminder that despite it being the year's snowiest month, better things lay ahead, she'd announced.

I certainly hoped so.

I narrowed my eyes at the crystal pendant, nestled again against my chest. Somehow it seemed to sparkle more than usual in the moonlight that cascaded through the window. Probably just my imagination, I told myself, returning my attention to the soup pot.

There were plenty of myths and legends surrounding the full moon, of course. Nursing friends had solemnly assured me that more babies made their appearance at the full moon then than at any other portion of the lunar cycle. The cops swore the full moon brought out the crazies in people.

I chuckled to myself. Maybe that's what had Devon the Dictator in such a foul mood tonight: the full moon. It was as good an explanation as any.

Setting the giant wooden spoon down on the spoonrest, I ducked into the pantry to hunt up the extra place settings Devon had ordered. Luckily, I discovered a top shelf holding just enough extra crockery to fill the bill. Mismatched patterns, but they'd have to do.

Clutching the stack of plates and glassware in my arms, I made my way through the kitchen to the dining room beyond, then scooted things around on the tables to accommodate the four additional settings. All was ready except finding four extra chairs and, since I had no idea where *those* were kept, I decided to leave that detail to His Annoying Highness to figure out.

I surveyed the tables with a critical eye, straightening a knife here and fork there; tugging the drooping corner of a folded napkin to make it stand at attention. On my way back to the kitchen my gaze snagged on a potted orchid on a stand near the kitchen door. One of the leaves had turned a paper-y brown, and the flowers were wilting. Tugging off the dead leaf, I promised myself I would give it some water before I left tonight.

Devon erupted through the kitchen door just as I was tugging off the leaf. Naturally.

"Fussing with the plants again? That's not what I pay you for!" His arms shot up, his voice a screech.

It was no use arguing, so I didn't bother to reply. His heated gaze burned my back as I retreated to the kitchen again. Picking up my soup spoon, I gave the pot an especially vigorous stir.

Hannah, my co-worker, turned a sympathetic eye my way as she prepped the salads but wisely said nothing. Devon stormed through the kitchen door, stopping just long enough to glare in my direction. Apparently satisfied to find me back in front of the stove, he turned on his heel and swept out again.

The comforting aroma of roast beef filled the kitchen. When I cracked the door of the second oven for a peek, the bread wore a golden crust. Dipping a smaller spoon in the giant pot, I sampled the carrot soup. Not bad at all. Velvety and smooth. A pinch more ginger would finish it to perfection.

Reaching for the spice tin, I frowned. A half-teaspoon would have done it. Maybe even less. But the tin was completely empty.

"I'm out of ginger, but I think I saw more in the pantry," I called to Hannah. "Be right back."

Mentally I crossed my fingers, hoping Devon the Devious wouldn't pick this exact moment to burst into the kitchen and find me gone.

As I turned toward the pantry an unexpected flash outside the window made me jump. An ominous roll of thunder followed, accompanied by the patter of heavy drops against the glass. The storm seemed to be gathering in intensity.

The luscious full moon was already well above the treetops and peeking through the clouds. Another unexpected burst of lightning and a near-instantaneous clap of thunder made me jump. I felt the hairs on the back of my neck prickle.

That one was *close*.

Swinging open the door to the pantry, I flicked on the light switch stepped back inside. I hadn't cooked here often enough to be familiar with where everything was kept, but the standing racks of metal shelving appeared well-organized. Below the shelf where I'd already found the extra plates and glassware stood a cluster of cut-glass salt and pepper shakers. But no other spices.

Standard restaurant supplies occupied another rack of shelving – giant Number 10 cans holding everything from tomatoes and beans to olives, artichokes, and coffee. Shoving a few cans aside I bent and peered into the shadowy recesses at the back, hoping to spot where the spices were kept. They must be here *somewhere*. . . .

Another sudden burst of lightning shook me. I hadn't realized the pantry had a window. But sure enough, the brilliant flash hit the room like a strobe. The fiery glare seemed to be everywhere at once, exploding off the glassware, the tins, the metal racks –

And then the overhead lights went out.

It was pitch black in the pantry – *beyond* pitch black. I couldn't even make out the faint glow of the moon. I held my hand up in front of my face. Nothing.

Slowly, carefully, I began backing toward the door. The last thing I needed was to back into the metal shelves by mistake, bringing a cascade of dishware and restaurant supplies down on my head. Hand fumbling behind me, I reached for the doorknob.

My fingers brushed against something solid. But it wasn't a smooth wall or wooden door.

I turned in surprise, though I still couldn't see whatever was now directly in front of me. The tips of my fingers trailed across—fabric. Soft. Warm. And yet with steel beneath it. A chest, rising and falling with breath.

A large hand enveloped my wrist, stilling my hand. A *male* hand. And a distinctly masculine voice to go with it.

"Hell's bells, woman, light a candle, would you?"

With a yelp of surprise, I pulled back. I flailed for the door, trying to push past the body that blocked my way. But all I succeeded in doing was crashing into a hard thigh.

Steadying hands found my shoulder, and that booming voice was beside my ear.

"Easy, there."

I pushed away. And finally, *finally* my fingers clasped the cool, familiar metal of the doorknob. Flinging the door open wide, I burst out into the kitchen, only to find the lights were out there, too.

Here, at least, the moon's giant orb cast a sufficient glow to find my way around. So unnervingly bright, in fact, that shadows danced in the room as the gusting wind blew the trees outside.

The sound of footsteps confirmed the man had followed me into the kitchen. Quickly, I put the center island between us.

"Who *are* you?"

His head swung slowly from one end of the room to the other. Then he retreated a half-step, as if disoriented.

He was a large man, easily topping six feet. Mid-thirties, if I had to guess by what I could see of his face in the moonlight, with broad shoulders and a chiseled jaw. Dark hair with a lock that seemed determined to flop in his eyes the same way mine did.

He took another tentative step forward and sniffed the air, apparently picking up the smell of food. Was that why he had been in the pantry? Was he homeless? Perhaps he was merely hungry.

I glanced around for my coworker, but Hannah was nowhere in sight.

Slowly, the man continued to approach. I backed up, keeping the island between us. I seized a knife from the chopping block and brandished it, trying to make myself as threatening as possible. "Don't come any closer!"

A low chuckle erupted. "There, there, no need for that. I mean you no harm." He stopped where he was and extended both hands, palms upward.

And for some strange reason, I believed him. If he'd intended to harm me, he would have done it in the pantry. He was moving slowly, as you would with a skittish animal. He hadn't tried to rush me.

I lowered the knife, keeping a tight grip on the handle, just in case.

The overhead lights flickered once then came on, flooding the kitchen with fluorescent brilliance. His head snapped up, mouth open. Then he took a step backward, his head swiveling slowly as he took in the commercial stove holding the soup pot. The giant stainless fridge. The ovens. The cappuccino-maker.

He lifted his chin, sniffing the air again. Was he a few letters shy of an alphabet?

"You. . . . This –" He swung his arms wide to encompass the kitchen. "Where am I? What *are* all these strange things?"

If anything was strange it was him. That wild shock of hair. His clothing. Like a photograph from a century or more ago, come to life. A longish jacket that covered his hips, with oddly narrow, notched lapels. White shirt with a thin collar, buttoned all the way to the neck. The flaps of his jacket hung open, revealing the flash of a gold watch chain. Boots that climbed his legs nearly to the knees. And a stiff-brimmed hat in a style I'd seen only in old movies or vintage photographs. A bolero I'd heard it called.

Though the jacket was dusty, the rest of his clothing seemed neat and his face was clean-shaven.

He had inched closer while I examined him and now stretched out a hand in slow motion. His fingers gently brushed my forearm.

I jumped as something like an electric shock ran through me.

He flinched, too, as if he'd seen a ghost. The man's mouth dropped open, revealing straight, white teeth. His eyes narrowed.

The shock on his face was strangely reassuring. He wasn't an intruder. And clearly he didn't mean anyone harm. So what was he doing here? And how the heck had he managed to walk past me and Hannah both to reach the pantry without being seen? The pantry window was too high in the wall for anyone to climb through, and it had no outside door.

I tried to think of something soothing to say. Instinctively, I reached out to touch his arm. Again, that sudden shock rocketed through me. I yanked my hand way.

A surge. A connection. Something deep. Almost like – recognition.

His head swung sharply toward the kitchen door. That's when I heard it, too. Pounding footsteps, headed our way. A rhythmic slap that could only be Devon's hard-heeled, polished-to-perfection loafers.

This time the surge I felt was bile, rising in my throat.

If Devon spotted us together in the kitchen he'd instantly leap to the catastrophically-wrong conclusion. He'd assume I'd brought a boyfriend to work, possibly to help steal something. Or perhaps we were just hanging out for a bit of hanky-panky. Even if he simply felt my mind wasn't one hundred percent on the job, that would translate to a fatal lack of loyalty in Devon's world. I'd be fired in a heartbeat.

I gulped down the bitter panic. I *couldn't* lose this job. Couldn't let Serena down. I was counting on tonight's paycheck.

"Quick! Follow me!" Grabbing the stranger by the hand I darted into the pantry again, ignoring whatever spark there was between us as I tugged him inside. I snicked the pantry door closed with my shoulder as quietly as I could and, with an elbow, toggled the light switch to douse the overhead fluorescents.

Darkness wrapped the pantry like a soothing blanket, though the full moon's glow pierced the high-up window and a narrow bar of light still edged the bottom of the door.

"What–?"

Tightening my fingers around his hand, pressed a cautioning finger to his lips. *"Shh!"* I hissed.

I forced myself to disregard the spark of – what *was* this exactly? warmth? electricity? – that ping-ponged between our hands.

The quick, determined footsteps slowed as they reached the pantry door. Stopped. Then kept going, fading away into the distance.

I released a breath I hadn't realized I was holding and gently squeezed the fingers still grasping mine.

Large fingers, I realized. Warm. With callouses that brushed my palm. I released my grip quickly, but didn't step away. Seconds ticked by. In some bizarre way, standing in the dark mere inches from this stranger's chest, our breaths mingling, felt exactly right.

"That was close. But I think he's finally gone." I kept it to a whisper.

Over his shoulder, I watched the full moon break free from the clouds to emerge in all its glory. Its color had morphed from pale silver earlier in the evening to a deep, burnt orange. And though I knew it wasn't possible, its orb appeared half again its normal size.

The clouds that had obscured the moon's face began scudding away, as if repelled by some strange magnetic force, leaving only the oversized ball to dominate the night sky. As I stared, the orange moon began to pulse, slowly growing brighter and sharper, then dimming and becoming hazy at the edges before slowly swelling to brilliant gold again.

That simply couldn't be. The moon didn't pulse.

I blinked, then blinked hard again. But the orange orb continued to swell and soften, advance and retreat. A visible heartbeat in the sky.

Suddenly a flash of lightning ripped through the dark sky, momentarily blinding me. I grabbed the stranger's arms. Seconds later, a roll of thunder crashed, as deep and foreboding as the trumpet blare of an advancing army.

A second burst of lightning followed; brighter than the first, if that were possible. It seemed to sizzle through the tiny pantry, generating an answering cascade of sparks from the glassware and metal shelving. A faint buzz at my chest drew my gaze lower – the crystal pendant, too, was suddenly afire, glowing as if with an other-worldly light.

Strong arms suddenly folded me protectively against a hard chest and in the half-second I had for conscious thought, I felt grateful for the comfort. Then our conjoined bodies were tossed as if by an unseen hurricane—tumbling, soaring, twirling through space, coasting, spinning in a way that left my head dizzy. . . before my world went black.

Chapter 2

LUCAS

I groaned. Cracking one eye open, I squinted upward. To see night sky between the tops of trees.

I was flat on my back, arms splayed wide. Everything from the soles of my feet to the top of my head felt bruised, as if I'd been shaken so hard the strings of my being had been torn free and the parts strangely reordered before being reattached.

Peeling my second eye open with some difficulty, I squinted upward again. The moon that peeked out from behind a swirl of clouds seemed extra-huge tonight, with an odd orange tinge. I'd seen that strange pumpkin moon someplace before, I thought, though my head was still too foggy at the moment to remember exactly where.

Slowly, I turned my head to the left. My hat must have fallen off when I fell, as there it lay, some distance away.

With another groan I tried to sit up. Only to realize a weight across my chest was pressing me down.

A body. A soft, *warm* body.

Gently, I levered myself up on my elbows and peered down. A woman. Her dark hair fanning out across my chest like a river of India ink. Eyes closed as if asleep, or possibly unconscious? Or – I swallowed hard. Something much worse?

I bent my head toward hers to check for breathing. Alive. She was definitely alive.

Even by the light of the moon I could see she was beautiful. No more than twenty-five, with a dimpled chin and sweet mouth. Dark eyelashes that formed twin arcs across her skin. A high, rounded forehead suggesting brains as well as great beauty.

I'd seen *her* someplace before, too, I thought. But when?

A haze of memories tickled my brain. I remembered ambling down to Glenbrook House tonight, pursuing nothing more serious than a drink at the tavern. Remembered seeing the familiar sawmills, puffing away in the distance. Hearing the occasional crack of thunder.

The clouds had been leaking raindrops then, but not enough to pose a serious inconvenience. Until I'd reached the back door, anyway. Just as I reached for the metal handle, the skies had opened up, loosing a wall of water across my hat and shoulders. A sudden flash of lightning had brought the scene into sharp relief: the soggy wooden porch, dilapidated door canting slightly on one hinge, sugar pine shakes curling up slightly at the ends. A second roll of thunder had followed the glare almost instantly.

That must've been close, I remember thinking. So close I'd caught a pungent whiff of sulphur. But before my fingers had even grasped the door handle, another gigantic flash of lightning had enveloped me. Like a thousand suns exploding in my face. So bright, I'd instinctively thrown an arm across my eyes.

I shook my head as the cobwebs receded further. It couldn't possibly have happened the way I remembered. And yet it had.

I remembered falling, as if the world had suddenly canted on its axis. As if the solid porch beneath my feet fell away and the earth was trying to swallow me up. And then there'd been darkness – the most perfect, utter blackness. Like a velvet cloak had been thrown over my head.

And finally, the feel of small fingers lightly tracing my chest. A woman's fingers, judging by the outcry that followed. I'd followed her out of that pitch-black room into another that was not quite as dark – a kitchen, judging by the smell. And definitely not the familiar kitchen of the tavern. I'd been there too many times getting a bone for my dog to mistake the difference. No, definitely not the kitchen I was used to.

Suddenly, strange lights had appeared in the ceiling. Not candles, not lanterns. I'd detected no visible flame. But the room had instantly become bright as day. And my jaw had dropped at the strange, otherworldly objects I saw filling it.

Old Hans' tired, cast-iron woodstove with its blackened chimney pipe were nowhere to be seen. The painted wooden cupboards – gone. Even the sour-smelling pine counters had disappeared, replaced by a smooth expanse of shiny metal. Polished silver, perhaps?

Gingerly I rolled flat again, settling my head back against the wet grass. The moon, barely visible through the trees, seemed to have recovered its normal size. But – I squinted, then blinked hard and squinted again. Was it still pulsing faintly?

No, it must be an illusion. It was the same familiar moon. Perhaps I *had* made it to the tavern after all and simply drank too much?

The ground beneath my hips was cold and damp, and freezing air whistled across my cheek. A fat drop of rain splatted on my forehead.

Groaning, I glanced down at the sleeping woman sprawled across my chest. She was pretty, I'd give her that. Though her clothing was outrageous. Why on earth would her legs be encased in men's trousers?! Though I had to admit they displayed her figure to advantage. A well-proportioned bosom, hips suggesting she'd been made for children. Just the sort of lush figure I'd be attracted to if –

Well. If things had gone better.

But they hadn't. Life, in fact, had gone to hell in a handbasket these past six months. I pushed the thought away.

All of which confirmed again that I should have been more like my younger brother. My *infinitely smarter* younger brother, who hadn't wasted five years, as I had, attempting to wrest a fortune from the bloody uncooperative Comstock mines.

Instead, slowly and steadily, my brilliant brother had built a cattle empire for himself over in the Central Valley. Found himself a nice, sweet wife and settled down. Produced two bouncing offspring; possibly three, judging by his most recent letter.

I, on the other hand, had pursued the silver dream with a vengeance, positive success would eventually come.

It hadn't. By the time I finally figured out that silver mining wouldn't be my ticket to riches, I'd been anxious to catch up. Fast. So when a chance had materialized to buy a timber ranch at Tahoe, I'd scraped together every penny I could for a down-payment.

Sylvester Sullivan, Tahoe agent for Bank of San Francisco, had made the land acquisition so easy. No payments at all for the first two years, then interest-only for another three years before the debt would finally come due. 'Friend' that he was, Sullivan also arranged for me to purchase a steamer to tow my timber across the lake to Pray's sawmill. And when an opportunity arose last year to pick up another thousand acres of prime timber land at the south end of the lake, I'd leapt at it. Sullivan had been only too ready to lend me the additional cash.

Now, of course, I was painfully over a barrel. Sullivan's carefully-crafted barrel, to be precise. The national depression had pulled the timber business into an economic sinkhole. I'd fallen behind on my payments. So far behind I had no real hope of catching up. And the future for timber had never looked worse.

That's what I got for going after my new dream so aggressively, hoping to show my brother that I, too, could make something of my life. That I'd moved on from the false glitter of mining to something much safer and far more rational. Huge fortunes had been made supplying the Comstock mines, after all, and those mines voraciously consumed timber. Always would. Timber had looked invincible as long as the Comstock was booming.

Not so invincible once the mines began to play out, however. Six or seven months ago I'd finally awoken to the realization that I had dug myself a huge financial hole.

About that same time, my intended had run off. At least, I *presumed* she'd run off. Amanda hadn't bothered to deliver the bad news to my face. Instead, one day when I'd paid a call she was simply gone. Along with her clothes, her fancy ribbons, even the diamond brooch I'd bought her.

The landlady had pursed her lips and shook her head in disgust. She had no idea whatsoever where Amanda had gone, she assured me. And no, Amanda hadn't left me a letter or a forwarding address.

Another burst of lightning lit up the night sky, as a fat raindrop crawled down my cheek.

A groan escaped my throat, but I couldn't bring myself to move just yet. Once things began to go wrong, another bundle of woes always joined in, right? Like a pack of wolves, assembling for the hunt. The prey? That would be me.

So just as the Comstock mines had begun to fade, the national recession had made further borrowing impossible. And Sullivan knew it. He'd been openly rubbing his hands together over the prospect I couldn't pay.

Surprisingly, Amanda's leaving had broken my heart far less than I would have expected. Sure, we'd been engaged to be married. And I'd kicked myself a thousand times for the financial predicament I found myself in. But in retrospect, perhaps Amanda's sudden disappearance was the one *lucky* thing that had happened recently.

Along with possibly meeting whoever this was, sprawled across my chest. I looked down again at those dark lashes, her ebony hair. Then quietly harrumphed. More likely she would prove one more unneeded complication in my already-unraveling life.

Something about her, though, awakened a long-dormant protective instinct. Raising one hand, I gently traced the backs of my fingers across her face. Those dark lashes fluttered in response.

With a start, her eyes popped open. She glanced around, a sudden frown creasing her brow. Hastily, she pushed herself off my chest and sat up, legs half-tucked beneath her.

In addition to those odd men's trousers, she wore a thin, fluffy sweater of a material I didn't recognize. A gem of some kind sparkled faintly in the moonlight from a chain around her neck. And her feet were laced into the strangest footwear I'd ever seen. Resembling fabric more than leather, they fluoresced slightly in the moonlight as she shifted position. None of her clothing offered nearly protection enough for the current frigid weather.

I, too, pushed myself to sitting, painfully aware of the wet, hard ground beneath my buttocks. The sharp breeze off the lake carried icicles.

My companion winced as a drop of moisture splatted against her face. Soon, sheets of rain would descend on us in earnest.

"Where am I?" she asked, glancing around in evident confusion.

"Behind the Station." That much I knew; the familiar stoop to the back door loomed only a few feet away. How we both got here, exactly, I had no idea. Last I remembered, I'd been *on* that stoop, about to enter. And where on earth had she been?! "You have a room here?"

Her frown simply deepened.

"Are you staying here? At the inn?"

Her answer was a puzzled shake of her head. "I have no idea what you're talking about. I live at Tahoe."

I simply pointed. "This is the Glenbrook House."

Her eyes widened. Had she fallen and hit her head?

"Where exactly is your home? Shall I hire a buggy to take you there?"

She shook her head again, frown deepening.

I pushed myself to my feet, retrieved my hat and slapped it back on my head. I extended a hand to help the woman up. Reluctantly she took it, wincing slightly as she stood. The ground had been hard indeed. A sudden rustle in the bushes to my left caused my head to swing around. Was someone there? Had somebody been watching us as we reclined together so intimately on the ground? A moment of panic washed through me. There was no good way of explaining our position.

But no figure emerged from the bushes. The shadows remained still. Simply a gust of the wind rustling dead leaves, I told myself. Except that my companion seemed to have heard the same noise. Her head swung slowly back and forth, as if searching for the source of the sound. Her gaze swept back toward the inn, then focused back on me.

Hastily she dropped my hand, a moment of suspicion lighting her eyes. Then her face relaxed as if concluding I posed no threat.

Her lips wrinkled in disgust as she brushed her palms against her trousers. "All this looks so unfamiliar I'm not even sure which direction home *is*, right now."

Alright, I told myself. She's lost and confused. Maybe she *did* hit her head. But that was something we'd have to sort out in the morning. Right now we had more immediate things to worry about. The patter of occasional drops had turned into a steady drizzle. Soon, we'd be soaked.

"Come on," I said, gently taking her arm. "My cabin isn't far away."

She planted her feet. "But my sister! I have to get back!" Panic laced her voice.

"You can't simply stay out here all night. We need to get you warm. We'll deal with it in the morning."

I took her arm again, and this time she allowed me to lead her to the road. Her head bobbed as we walked: studying the trees lining the dirt track, the moon surging in and out of swirling clouds overhead. It was late enough no lamplight glowed from the windows of the handful of cabins we passed.

"We're still at the Lake, right?" Her voice sounded small.

"Of course." She *had* hit her head, I thought. "The lake's over there, through the trees." I pointed to our left.

"I can't believe it! Where are the cars? The street lights? The homes?"

The toe of her strange footgear hit a stone and she stumbled slightly, tugging heavily on my arm.

A moment later she huffed and dropped my arm. "This is some kind of joke, right? There's a video crew waiting in the trees, ready to turn on the klieg lights and yell 'Gotcha!'"

What on earth was she raving about? She certainly employed some odd figures of speech.

Not knowing how to answer, I didn't bother to respond. A cup of tea and the warmth of a fire – that's all I had to offer. I hoped it would be enough.

The rain had let up for the time being, but the wind was still gusting. It wouldn't be long before the clouds opened up again.

I picked up the pace a bit. Luckily, she matched it without arguing.

A few minutes later she touched my forearm. That wrinkle had appeared in her forehead again. She leaned closer, as if studying my hat, then my boots. Strangely enough, she was looking at me as if *I* might be the crazy one.

"What year is this?"

"Eighteen eighty-seven, of course."

Her fingers slid away, her mouth open. "You're kidding, right?"

"No. Why?"

My mind was racing. It wasn't possible. But then again, it would explain so much. "What year do *you* think it should be?"

"Twenty twenty-three." She said it matter-of-factly.

My mouth went dry.

A few paces later the trees on our left opened up, revealing the shining white Tallac Cross on the mountains across the lake. She stopped, staring.

"This definitely *is* Tahoe, then." I heard her swallow, hard. "The lake, the Cross – it's all the same. I can't believe it. But somehow it seems I've jumped 130-odd years back in time."

Frankly I couldn't believe it either. A smack to the head made a much more logical explanation. Or perhaps she simply was off her rocker. And yet –

Turning my gaze forward again, I gave her arm a tug. My cabin wasn't much further. And the night wasn't getting any warmer.

Ideas kept spinning in my head as we walked, her strides matching mine. A leap through time? What a totally crazy idea. But then again, what if it were true? That would explain her outrageous garb. The impossible fluorescence of her oddly-designed shoes. Her strange manner of speech.

"Who's the president now?" She turned that pretty face up to look at me.

"Grover Cleveland, of course. His second term." I tried to swallow quietly. "Who do you think is president?"

Shaking her head, she looked away. "You've never heard of him."

A gust of wind brought a fresh burst of rain with it. Removing my outer jacket, I threw it over her shoulders and together we broke into a run. "It's not much farther," I urged, pleased she was able to match my pace. Perhaps there was something utilitarian in her odd choice of clothing, after all. Footwear without a fashionable high stacked heel. No skirts tangling about her legs.

"Could it have something to do with the full moon?" she huffed as we ran. "It's still February, right?"

I nodded.

"They call it the Snow Moon, at least where I'm from," she continued. "A symbol of hope. The promise of happy changes ahead."

Her fingers held my jacket, clutching the lapels tight over her head. Together, our feet made tandem splashes in the puddles dotting the road. "You saw the moon pulsing earlier tonight, right?"

I gave a short nod, not quite ready to talk about that oddly pulsing moon. "I remember seeing a sudden flash of lightning just as I was about to enter the inn."

"So that *was* you in the pantry and kitchen. I remember you looking around –"

I pressed my lips together. I remembered, too. Those smooth, silvery countertops. The otherworldly lights overhead. Whatever those bizarre, unidentified contraptions might have been lining the walls.

"Until another flash," she continued. "My necklace had been glowing just before it hit. Somehow I'm guessing when you got drawn back in time, I came with you. Where we landed was probably the exact same spot where the pantry will eventually be built a century-plus from now."

It made perfect sense. Crazy, illogical, perfect sense. I remembered her hand on my arm when that final burst of lightning hit. So if there *was* some kind of full-moon magic at work, it enveloped both of us.

"But I really need to get back to my own time. My sister – she'll be worried." She threw me a glance. "I'm her guardian. Our parents died last year. She's only seventeen." Then she chuckled, a low, throaty sound that sparked a surprising answering warmth in my belly. I could listen to that laugh all day. "Well, seventeen going on thirty, if you know what I mean."

I couldn't help but smile. Some things apparently hadn't changed, even in a hundred and thirty years.

Our footsteps continued to slap out a watery tattoo on the muddy road.

"My condolences on losing both your parents." It wasn't quite the right thing to say. It didn't feel like enough. But I didn't know what else to say.

"As far as reversing whatever this spell you've experienced – I'm afraid we'll have to figure it out later."

Right now it was bitterly cold, and the downpour seemed to be intensifying. Luckily, my cabin lay just ahead at the edge of the meadow.

I broke stride as we finally reached it to push open the door for her, and we both burst inside, breathing hard. Small puddles formed at our feet as rainwater dripped from our hair and clothing. Slamming the door behind us, I reached for the stub of candle I kept beside the door, and struck a match. The candle flared to life, and I touched it to the two hanging oil lamps, their twin pools adding welcome light in the dim interior.

Hasty must have been asleep in his usual spot in the corner before we arrived, but was already on his feet, coming to greet me, tail wagging. That excited, happy look on his face that only dogs seem to have mastered. I bent to ruffle the fur between his ears.

"And who's this?" She bent, slowly extending the back of her hand for him to sniff.

"Careful –" My arm was already in motion to stop her, but surprisingly it didn't prove necessary. Hasty, growler *extraordinaire*, the one-man dog who treated all strangers as a clear and present danger until proven otherwise, had just burrowed his snout companionably in the woman's fingers and lowered his head for a scratch.

"Such a good dog! What's his name?"

Huh. I watched in disbelief as the tempo of his tail-wag accelerated and he rubbed his white-and-black speckled flank against her legs.

"Hasty. Short for Hasty Pudding," I managed at last.

Her eyes landed on my face, her lips twisted in a grin. "There must be a story there."

"He, uh, managed to get into a bowl of hasty pudding left on the table when he was a pup."

Her smile never wavered.

"English setter?"

She knew her dogs. I nodded.

"He's so cute with the one black ear." She was down on one knee, now. Hasty took full advantage by settling his head across her thigh, eyes drifting half-closed as she scruffed the fur around his ears and jaw.

The traitor.

"So, this is your cabin?" Her head swung up and around, taking in the single, rustic room with its cast-iron woodstove dominating the center. "What do you do for a living?"

"I'm in the timber business." I lowered myself into a wooden chair and began to tug off my sopping boots. "And I have a boat here on the lake. Name's Lucas Russell. And you are?"

"Rachel Moretti."

She didn't preface it with "Miss" or "Mrs.," so I stole a surreptitious glance at her left hand. *Miss* Moretti, apparently.

"Welcome to my humble abode."

Her head swung around slowly, taking in the woodstove and the stack of logs on the hearth; the corner desk with bookshelf above; the table that served as pantry, kitchen and dining room combined; Hasty's blanket in the corner. And the bed. Her gaze lingered there for a split second too long before she blinked and returned her gaze to me.

"So, we're guessing it must have been the storm—the lightning—that brought me here with you. Any idea about how I can get home again?"

I turned my back and set about adding a fresh log to the fire.

"Aren't you going to answer me?"

"Miss Moretti." I hoped my voice sounded less irritated than I felt. "I seriously have no idea how to get you back where you belong. Though like you, I do hope it'll happen soon."

I heard a faint huff behind me. I hadn't meant to annoy her, but I certainly had no magic answers about the crazy energy that may have brought her here. Or brought me *there* and back again, for that matter.

I had enough troubles on my hands without trying to sort out someone else's. I wasn't doing terribly well unraveling the knots in my own life. I could hardly have left her where I found her, out in the cold rain. But now what?!

Craning my head over my shoulder, I glanced at my bed against the wall. That was going to be a whole other problem. Now *my* problem, too.

It wasn't like I was anxious to make her feel bad. It wasn't her fault she got here. But yeah. We needed to find some way to propel her back where she belonged.

I had troubles enough of my own, thank you very much.

The fire sprang to life, orange-yellow flames licking the edges of the dry wood I'd added. Satisfied, I turned on my haunches, one arm braced against the floor.

"You can take the bed tonight. I'll make a pallet under the window. It's not much privacy, I know." I swept an arm around the tiny cabin. "But we'll just have to make the best of it."

She wrapped her arms around herself as if considering my suggestion, then bit her lip and gave a short nod. "That's very kind of you. But I can take the floor."

I rose. "It's late, and it'll soon be freezing out. You can have the bed. It's only for one night."

She looked as if she were about to protest again. Then I saw it in her eyes when reality dawned. Where would she go if she left?! Of course I was right. For better or for worse, there was no way I could throw her out. I was only being as much of a gentleman as present circumstances permitted, which really wasn't much.

She nodded finally. An unspoken truce. "Well, I'll just say thanks, then."

Taking a seat in the chair I had just vacated, she began to unlace those queer many-hued shoes. I watched, stunned again at the notion I might be looking at someone from the future.

Well, if the full moon really had something to do with it, perhaps the next full moon would send her back. I gritted my teeth. Even if that were possible, though, it meant we would be stuck together for another month at minimum. But unexpected visitor or no, my honor wouldn't let me simply cast her out.

She'd finished untying her shoes and removed her socks next, stretching her toes toward the fire. Perhaps she felt my gaze on her; she looked up. Our eyes met in the soft lamplight. Her brow was still furrowed, her lips tight.

"If you're worried about your reputation or the nature of my intentions, don't. We both need sleep, that's all. The bed's yours. Just get some rest. We can talk more in the morning."

I pulled a pair of blankets from my trunk, folding them into a thickness I hoped would soften the hard wood floor enough to get me through the night. Hasty came over to inspect my efforts before retreating to his own familiar bed in the corner and curling up.

"Ready?" I called over my shoulder as I lifted the globe to pinch out the final light.

"I guess."

The cabin plunged into darkness. Not total darkness, of course; the full moon still lent a faint glow through the window. Enough to make out rough shapes, if not details.

I heard the swish of fabric as she bent and stripped off those wildly inappropriate trousers. Saw the outline of her lithe figure bend to lift the covers on the bed, then slide beneath the heavy blanket.

"Goodnight, then," she said. A whisper.

What could I do but answer?

"Good night."

Knowing full well it was going to be anything but a good night on this hard floor. Settling in as best I could, I turned to face the wall.

The faint *tip-tap-tip* of doggie toenails a few minutes later made me lift my head to see what was happening.

I suppressed a groan. My formerly loyal companion had abandoned his own bed to cuddle up with Rachel in mine! She apparently welcomed his company; she'd wrapped one arm around his neck.

I turned back to face the wall again, spending the next hour trying in vain to find a comfortable position. My unexpected roommate, however, was soon breathing deeply and steadily. And Hasty, as usual, was flat-out snoring.

As the night wore on, the patter of rain against the window above my head faded to nothingness. A sign that the rain had probably turned to snow.

Time travel. Miss Rachel Moretti in trousers. A full moon and some bizarre kind of magic. A kitchen of the future I had beheld with my very own eyes.

Unlike either of my companions, it took me well into the night to sink into the blessing of sleep.

Sunlight was streaming enthusiastically through the window by the time I opened my eyes. But it wasn't the bright light that had awakened me. Instead, it was a loud pounding at the front door.

I threw back the blankets of my makeshift pallet and reached for my trousers where I'd tossed them over a chair. A stolen glance over my shoulder confirmed my unintended roommate was still abed, despite the racket. As I watched, one sleepy arm reached out, tugging the covers up more tightly around her neck.

Hasty, though, was not only awake but had already leaped to the floor. I finished hurriedly buttoning my trousers while, behind me, Hasty issued a throaty growl. I turned to shush him and found my dog, guard hairs raised and all four legs braced, at the foot of the bed.

Forget about any potential danger to me. The furry traitor was primed and ready to take on any threats to *Rachel.*

"Hush," I ordered more grumpily than I intended, cracking open the door.

"A warm good mornin' to you!" sang out my visitor, blue eyes twinkling at his ironic allusion to warmth. Despite the sun's bright rays, a thin white coat of snow carpeted the ground and the air was anything but toasty. His breath formed swirling clouds as he spoke.

Like me, A.J. Todman commanded a ship at Tahoe. Unlike my utilitarian craft, however, Todman's was fitted out as a pleasure steamer. He also ran a local fish hatchery that, if you believed the local paper, was set to release over a million trout into the waters of Tahoe this spring.

"Good morning to you, too," I growled, keeping the crack in the doorway as narrow as I could. "What brings you to my door so early?"

"Early?! It's half-past eight!" he chortled. "Since when are you a lay-abed?!"

His eyes slid over my shoulder and his grin slowly widened, wrinkling his leathered face. "Ah, sorry mate. Didn't realize ye had . . . *company.*"

He'd spotted Rachel. Asleep. In my bed.

I choked back a handful of choice cuss words.

"Not company, exactly." I ran one hand through my hair, then ad libbed the first excuse that sprang to mind. "That's, uh, my wife. We were just married. Up in Virginia." Pulling back hastily, I made to close the door. "So if you wouldn't mind excusing us –"

"Well, well!" Todman's hands came up in mock surrender. "My heartiest congratulations!" He stretched out a meaty paw. Leaning forward, I shook perfunctorily, adding what I hoped resembled a happy grin. Then slammed the door on his retreating form.

And felt the burn of eyes on my back.

I turned. Rachel sat upright in bed, eyes wide and covers clutched to her chest. And a look of utter horror on her face.

What on earth had I just done?!

Chapter 3

RACHEL

The noise of the slamming door echoed in the hard-walled cabin.

"Excuse me, did I hear you right? Did you just call me your *wife?*"

My fists tightened on the covers. Part of me wishing they were curled around his neck instead.

Padding over, Hasty took that opportunity to give my cheek a good-morning wash.

Lucas had the good grace to look sheepish, but he didn't immediately answer me. Just ran his fingers through all that glorious hair and turned his back, reaching for a shirt draped across the chair. Despite myself, I couldn't help but admire his bare torso, tapering from broad, muscular shoulders to a trim waist.

I pressed my lips together, irritated at my own thoughts for going there. Just another sign that since I took over Selena's care I hadn't had time for romance, I supposed.

I narrowed my eyes at his admittedly stellar masculine back. "We definitely need to talk." I was still too sleepy to mount a concerted verbal attack at this precise moment, unfortunately.

Lucas didn't react. Maybe he didn't *have* a good answer. But how annoying! He continued threading his arms into the sleeves of his shirt as if nothing had happened.

As I watched, he rummaged in a trunk in the corner, pulling out a heavy, knitted sweater. Tugged it over his head. Strode to a ceramic pitcher and bowl on a stand nearby and splashed water on his face. Then, seating himself on the same chair where his clothes had hung, he began lacing up his boots.

"There's coffee over there if you want it." A short toss of his head directed my attention to a shelf on the wall. "And there's a bit of bread and cheese on the table."

Reluctantly, I swung my gaze to the shelf. Coffee? Now he was speaking my language!

I spied a tall tin that presumably held ground beans, and a black kettle. No Mr. Coffee machine, of course. Guess if I wanted a morning brew I'd have to figure out how to make the coffee magic happen 1887-style.

I thought briefly about getting up to demand answers about his bizarre statement at the door. But my second thought reminded me I'd slept in just my bra and underwear.

I glanced longingly at my pile of clothes in a heap on the floor, where I'd ditched them in the dark last night. Lucas seemed to be getting ready to leave. I'd have to just bide my time.

He was standing now, folding the blankets he had slept on. He ran a comb through his hair, then grabbed his hat from the peg by the front door, turning its brim nervously in his fingers.

"Got a raft of wood to get across the lake today. But I should be home before dark." He shifted his weight, his gaze swiveling to my pile of garments on the floor. "I'll see if I can't rustle up some better clothes for you while I'm out."

I shrugged. "Not to worry. They should be dry enough now. I'll just wear my own."

His eyes twinkled, lips turning up in the first genuine smile I'd seen. "Not a good idea unless you're eager to be laughed out of Tahoe. A woman in pants?" He chuffed as if the notion was insanely ridiculous. "There's a fella I know near the dock, just got married. His wife's about your size, I think. I'll see if I can't borrow a dress and a few –" He stopped abruptly, the tips of his ears turning slightly red. "A few *other* things for you. I'll tell them you just got in yesterday, and your luggage was stolen in Virginia."

I wrinkled my lips. Dresses really weren't my thing. Especially down-to-your-ankles, Victorian-style dresses. With a corset, most likely.

But he was right. If I didn't intend to stand out like a sore thumb I'd have to get used to them. For now, at least. Surely it wouldn't be long before I'd figure out a way back to my own life.

Grudgingly, I nodded. "Thanks. You're right. I probably don't need to attract any more attention than I just did. Who was that fellow at the door?"

"A fellow boat captain. Goes by A.J., but Todman's his last name. Owns the Tod Goodwin, a pleasure craft on the Lake." He sucked in his lower lip and paused for a second. "Once he saw you I didn't know what else to say." It was as close as I was going to get to an apology.

Because, of course, girlfriends and sleepovers didn't happen in 1887. At least, nobody would admit it if they did.

"Aren't people going to ask how you came by a wife all of a sudden?"

He lifted a shoulder. "Yeah. They probably will." His eyes slid over my mussed-up hair and there was that smile again, though he didn't say anything.

Shoot. My hand flew to my messy locks. Morning was never my best look.

Which reminded me, now I'd have to figure out how to do something period-appropriate with my hair, too. How exactly *did* women wear long hair in 1887? Braids? A school teacher-ish bun? I wasn't sure I could pull off either look, especially without benefit of elastic bands.

Hair made me think of Selena, always so fashion-forward with her hairstyles and colors. What was she doing this morning? Was she panicking? Had she even missed me?

I assumed time was elapsing at the same rate for her as I was experiencing it here. But that was merely a guess. When I finally *did* find my way back to 2023, was it possible only seconds would have passed?

Lucas set his hat down on the chair. Tucked his pants legs, one at a time, into his tall boots. Stuffed his arms into the sleeves of a heavy mackinaw. Then clapped the hat on his head again.

"You'll stay here 'til I get back, yes?" It was more an order than a question. But there was a note of genuine concern in his voice.

The thought of obeying irked me, especially when he was being so grumpily distant. But he *had* given me a place to stay last night. And really, where would I go if I left? A glance out the window showed a white, frosty world.

Reluctantly, I nodded. "Fine. But when you get back tonight, we definitely need to talk."

He had the good grace to look uncomfortable. "Yeah. I kinda opened my mouth there with old A.J."

"So, is that really a problem? Will he repeat that *wife* remark to anybody?"

Lucas huffed out a laugh. "Only everybody in Glenbrook. A.J.'s the village busybody. But it was the only solution I could think of at the time. Guess we'll have to come up with some cock-and-bull story about how we met. At least until we can get you home."

My stomach fell. So I was expected to follow through with the charade he'd concocted?

I mean, I got it. 'Reputation' was everything in the Victorian era; he'd been trying to protect mine. His motives had been good, anyway. I had to give him that. Whether it really would be an issue all depended on how long I would be here, I reminded myself. Which, at this exact moment, I had no way of knowing.

"Make yourself comfortable." His hand swept the interior of the cabin. "But it would be better if you don't go outside to be seen in –" a finger indicated my pile of clothing on the floor "– those."

With a nod, Lucas let himself out, Hasty trotting at his heels.

And the door clicked shut behind them.

Chapter 4

RACHEL

I was alone in a strange and yet oddly familiar place.

Through the window, Lake Tahoe sparkled in the distance. Unlike everything else, those crystal blue waters and the mountains in the distance hadn't changed at all.

I was the one usually "on top of my game." I made things happen. Found answers to problems. Figured out what needed to be figured, and handled it. But here? I felt oddly discombobulated.

I found myself wishing Lucas hadn't left, even though talking clearly wasn't his forte. He had business to attend to. And it wasn't as if we were *friends*, after all.

But he'd seemed kind. And he was the only person in this whole, strange version of the world who knew where I'd actually come from. Or more accurately, *when*.

I wasn't just out of my element. I was out of place. Out of sync. Out of *time*. And aside from waiting around another four weeks for the next full moon, I had zero bright ideas about how to get back.

Well, moping certainly wasn't going to do it.

I threw back the covers and tugged on my clothes. At least *they* were familiar. Then, arms crossed, I spun slowly in a circle, surveying my surroundings.

The one-room cabin was small but neat. Closer inspection disclosed a fine layer of dust on the windowsill. On *everything*, really. And more than a few cobwebs in the corners.

The central woodstove dominated the room, its cast-iron legs set on a small brick hearth. The long shelf with the tin of coffee also held assorted canned goods, spices, a glass jar that looked like honey, and a short stack of china plates and bowls.

Against the opposite wall sat the narrow bed where I'd slept, a weathered seaman's chest at the foot and a small table to one side. A pair of boots languished beside the front door, soles caked with mud. A crude broom and dustpan were propped stiffly in a nearby corner. And on the far wall was the wooden stand holding a bowl and pitcher where Lucas had washed up this morning.

To my surprise, a small writing desk occupied the remaining corner, with a short line of books arranged on a shelf above. I leaned closer to peer at the titles. Alongside tomes on nautical lore and the mechanical arts were Mark Twain's *Adventures of Huckleberry Finn* and Dan DeQuille's *History of the Big Bonanza.* I pulled that last volume down, releasing a cloud of dust in the process. Sneezing, I hastily replaced the book in its spot.

It finally struck me: the most basic amenity I was used to in a house was missing. I turned another complete circle. Nope. No sink. No plumbing of any kind. And in what was fast becoming a more urgent quest, no bathroom.

Striding over to the bed I lifted the dangling covers and bent to peer beneath the metal frame. Yup, a white ceramic chamber pot stood silently at the ready. If I ever went outside, I'd probably see the regulation wooden outhouse out back.

The thought made me shiver. Luckily, Lucas had left me a cheerful fire in the stove. But the outhouse would be unheated. Not exactly an enticing idea on a morning as cold as this.

Crossing my fingers that Lucas wouldn't come barging through the door after something he'd forgotten, I availed myself of the chamber pot and vowed to empty it outside in the outhouse just as soon as it got a little warmer. Emulating Lucas, I splashed water from the pitcher into the bowl, then cupped my palms to bring it to my face. If I wasn't already one hundred percent awake that would definitely have done the trick – that water was *cold!* I wiped my hands on the thin cotton towel hanging on a rack to one side.

I caught my reflection in the small mirror above the washstand and had to laugh. My hair was a fright, indeed! I hunted around for a brush or comb I might borrow temporarily. Sure enough, a comb was stashed in the washstand's drawer.

Working slowly, I vanquished the worst of my tangles and even managed a loose braid. Fingers pinching the end, I hunted for something to secure the braid with. Standing on tiptoe, I scanned every shelf. Nothing.

My eyes finally settled on the trunk at the foot of the bed. Lucas had pulled a shirt from that trunk this morning. Perhaps it also held a handkerchief or other scrap of cloth?

Releasing the braid – I would just have to fix it again – I knelt to tug open the trunk lid. Inside, the top-most item was a small metal box. I didn't mean to pry, but a quick glance told me it held only papers inside; some sort of loan documents, it looked like. Setting the box to one side, I dove deeper. Underneath was an assortment of men's clothing, all neatly folded. But no handkerchief, scrap of cloth, or anything else I could use as a hair tie.

I returned the metal box to its spot, closed the trunk lid, and kept looking. Eventually, my patience was rewarded. Behind a lower door on the washstand was a stack of clean, neatly-folded cotton rags. Bingo!

Notching the frayed edge on a rag with my teeth, I tore off a narrow strip, rolled it into a tie, and secured the end of my messy braid. I allowed myself a small breath of satisfaction. Now for breakfast.

I polished off the bread and cheese Lucas had left out on the table, then eyed the kettle. Stoking up the woodstove proved easy enough; a small heap of firewood lay handy on the hearth.

I took a guess and wandered outside in search of water and - other essentials. Sure enough, a long-handled pump stood sentry beside the cabin while, out back, the narrow, pointed roof of an outhouse rose from a cluster of bushes. I grabbed the kettle, and discovered a few hard pulls at the pump produced enough water to fill it. The water seemed fresh and clear as it splashed into the kettle, but I could only imagine what non-EPA-approved organisms it might be carrying. Good thing I'd be boiling it, I told myself. Then laughed. This well water was probably far more pure than the heavily-filtered, chlorine-laced brew that spilled from my kitchen tap.

Setting the kettle atop the woodstove to heat, I sat down to wait. Soon it was boiling merrily, a narrow chimney of steam curling up from the spout.

I prowled to the shelf to investigate the coffee tin. Another puff of dust flew as I removed the lid. Luckily, the coffee inside proved fresh and already finely ground. I snatched up the mug, spoon and strainer lying beside the tin, then rubbed an exploratory finger over the shelf itself. Yup, it had definitely been a while since anyone bothered to clean.

I dumped a generous spoonful of grounds into the kettle and settled the strainer over the mug. Coffee was coffee. I'd live with the result. I gave the brew three or four minutes to simmer, then poured myself a cupful and leaned back in the wooden chair, steaming mug in hand.

Lucas was probably right; best not to go meandering the neighborhood in my definitely-not-period-appropriate clothes. That meant I was pretty well stuck inside the cabin. What on earth could I do to kill time?

As the caffeine kicked in, an idea struck me: the least I could do to try to repay Lucas' hospitality. Swallowing the dregs (not bad, for my first woodstove brew!) I grabbed a handful of rags from the washstand and set to work. After wiping every shelf and surface clean, I lined the books up by spine height and straightened the spices, then swept out the grit and cobwebs as best I could with the broom.

Aside from the books there weren't many clues to Lucas' personality. Until I got to the bedside table, that is. There was a framed photograph of an older woman – possibly his mother. Beside it lay an old-fashioned bank passbook. That was definitely his business; I wiped the cover but didn't open it. Beneath lay a stack of letters, addressed to 'Mr. Lucas Russell, Glenbrook' in a feminine hand. A velvet-and-lace ribbon was tied around them.

Huh. Did Lucas have a girlfriend? None of my business, of course, though for some reason the thought bothered me. I wiped away the dust, then replaced everything just as I had found it.

After straightening the covers on the bed where I'd slept, I started in on the cabin's two front windows. Oh, what I wouldn't have given for a bottle of glass cleaner! But a vigorous wipe with a wet rag followed by polishing with a dry one left the panes better than when I started.

Finally, after peeking outside to ensure the coast was clear, I toted the dirty boots around back, smacking the soles together to knock off the caked-on mud, then polished them as best I could with a dry rag before replacing them by the front door.

It was late afternoon when Lucas pushed through the front door with Hasty at his heels. Sunlight spearing through the newly-cleaned front windows brought his torso into sharp relief as he tugged off his mackinaw and tossed it on a peg. I was still a bit torqued about being left alone all day, but tired and surprisingly satisfied with what I'd been able to accomplish.

I couldn't help but admire the broad stretch of his shoulders as he whipped off his hat, his brown hair glinting in the sun.

Lucas Russell was definitely a handsome man. With looks like that, it was surprising he wasn't married. Perhaps those letters held the answer. Though he would have been much handsomer without the frown clouding his forehead.

Lucas pivoted slowly. I grinned, expecting a compliment for my hard work.

Instead, annoyance flashing in those bright blue eyes. "I never asked you to clean my cabin."

My voice rose in indignation.

"I was trying to help!"

"Let me put it another way." His glare deepened. "I don't *want* you to clean my cabin."

So. That dust held deep, personal meaning to him? He didn't want anyone touching his precious stuff? What was he so afraid of? Did he think I'd read his letters?

Or was there something else he was hiding?

"*Sooo* sorry! I'll see what I can do to put the cobwebs back!" Sarcasm. It was my middle name sometimes.

He didn't respond right away. Folding his large frame into the hard wooden chair, he tossed a paper-wrapped package on the nearby table, then began to unlace his boots.

"As I promised. That's for you."

His eyes never met mine. If that was a present, he was certainly less than gracious about it.

Lucas bent forward, fingers working at a knot in his laces. As I watched, a great drop of blood splatted from his hand to the floor. The knuckles of his right hand were raw.

"You're hurt!"

Kneeling beside the chair, I reached for his hand. "What happened?"

He yanked his arm away. "Nothing to worry about." But a moment later he muttered, "Bring me a clean rag, would you?"

He grabbed the requested item from me sullenly, wrapping it tight around his fist. In seconds, a red bloom stained the fabric. He glanced up. "It'll stop in a minute." But his frown deepened.

I huffed. Talk about Mr. Personality. Cold. Aloof. Super-grumpy. And now bound and determined to insist that a serious wound was nothing.

Those broad shoulders and icy blue eyes might be superficially appealing, I'd grant him that. But if I was ever in the market for a husband, which I wasn't, Lucas Russell would not be making my short list.

Stubborn idiot.

I grabbed his wrist. "Let me see."

This time he grimaced but didn't fight me. Gently, I unwrapped the blood-soaked rag.

His knuckles were a mass of bruises and abrasions, deep and raw. Near the thumb was a deep cut, a glimpse of white showing through. Bone.

"What on earth did you do? Looks like you got your hand caught in a meat-grinder."

Rewrapping the hand quickly, I applied pressure to the deepest wound.

"Log rolled over and got me." A quick shrug signaled embarrassment.

Hasty took up a silent post beside the chair, his brown eyes flickering between the two of us. He knew something was wrong. Lucas reached over with his good hand to give the dog's head a scruff.

Neosporin wasn't an option; that hadn't been invented yet. I wracked my brain for old-time home remedies. Finally, something clicked.

"Here, hold this," I instructed, positioning Lucas' left hand to keep pressure on the wound.

After dumping out the cold coffee, I refilled the kettle with fresh water from the pump and set it on the stove to boil. While the water was heating, I sliced up some onion and garlic, chopping it fine, then added honey and mashed the concoction with a fork to make thick paste. Bowl in hand, I grabbed for Lucas' injured hand.

He yanked it away.

"Just trust me, okay?"

"Why? That looks awful."

I set my lips.

"I may not be a doctor yet, but I know my way around first aid. And this is all we've got. Don't be a tough guy." I reached for his hand again.

His eyebrows shot up. Woman apparently didn't speak that way to men in 1887. But this time he didn't fight me.

Carefully, I unwrapped the wound and dabbed at his hand and fingers with a clean rag dipped in the boiled water, washing away the dried blood. He winced slightly, but didn't object. Blood still oozed from the deepest wound, but the pressure seemed to have slowed it down a bit. Gently I began applying the gooey mixture with my fingers.

He pulled his hand away again. "You think that crazy concoction is going to keep it from putrifying?" He might as well have been asking if I seriously believed the moon was made of green cheese.

Thankfulness and appreciation obviously played no part in this man's psyche.

"That wound is down to the bone. You want to cop an attitude and die from infection?" I looked him square in the eye. "Go ahead. Be a hard-head."

His lips thinned. I could see mental gears turning in his head. He probably *had* seen someone who died from infection. It wouldn't have been a pretty sight.

He gave me an eye-roll but extended his hand again. Slowly, just to be difficult. A smile crept up his lips. It looked suspiciously like approval.

"I can tell you're not going to leave me alone 'til you get your way."

I finished applying a thick layer of the homemade antibiotic to his wounds, then wrapped his hand in a clean rag, securing it with a thin strip and knotted tied tightly. It probably hurt like the dickens, but Lucas said nothing.

"We'll clean it again tomorrow and apply more salve," I clapped him on the shoulder. His scowl was back. Definitely *not* agreeing.

Slowly, he raised his bandaged hand to his nose and sniffed. "That ought to keep the bears away tonight."

Hasty did the same, stretching his nose forward to inspect his master's strange new adornment. He pulled back sharply once he got a good sniff.

"See? Even Hasty disapproves."

"Just give it a week. You'll see."

Lucas merely huffed.

True, I'd never actually tried this particular remedy before, but I'd read about it. And it stood to reason it should help. Onion, garlic and honey all had proven antibiotic properties. And what other options did we have? We weren't going to come up with penicillin in 1887.

Toeing off his boots, Lucas stood in his stockinged feet.

"You might want to open that." He pointed a finger at the paper-wrapped package on the table.

"No worries. You're welcome," I spit. Irritating, stubborn man that he was, he'd merely changed the subject.

For a second I was tempted to ignore the package. But curiosity got the better of me. It turned out to contain the clothes he'd promised to borrow. Two pretty dresses - the right size, it looked like, plus a few underthings. Even a long flannel nightgown.

"Think they'll fit?" He quirked an eyebrow.

I nodded, fighting a smile. Apparently he'd paid more attention to my body than I'd realized.

"These should do just fine." It pained me, but politeness compelled me to add: "Thanks."

One of us needed to try to maintain some civility.

With a grunt he turned his back and began stoking the woodstove with one hand.

"You want help with that?"

"No thanks."

To my chagrin he did, in fact, manage just fine. Without a word he also whipped up dinner in a skillet on the woodstove - some sort of cured sausage I wasn't sure I wanted to inspect too closely. Potatoes, onions, a few spices. All fried together in bacon grease, judging by the aroma that filled the cabin.

It was filling, it was heavy, and it was oh so tasty. Probably two thousand calories and enough cholesterol to clog every single artery overnight. But so wonderful I asked for seconds.

I wiped my mouth on the cloth napkin he'd provided. "Thanks. You're a pretty good cook."

Lucas just shrugged again. His signature move, apparently.

His attention was fixed on Hasty. And Hasty's eyes were fixed on Lucas' nearly-empty plate. With two fingers, Lucas fished out a piece of sausage and tossed it the dog's direction.

Hasty gulped it down mid-air and continued staring. He wanted seconds, too.

When both our plates were empty, I reached out a hand for his. "You cooked. I'm happy to do dishes."

"Don't worry. I can manage." Snatching up the plates he disappeared through the front door. A few minutes later he returned with the plates dripping wet but clean.

Amazingly, he'd somehow managed to keep his bandaged hand dry. Thank heavens for small favors. I wasn't looking forward to a battle over treating it again.

"I could've done that."

"No need. You've done enough." It sounded more like an accusation than gratitude.

I let a beat go by, unsure how to respond.

"Listen, Lucas. I didn't ask to be brought here, and I'm not any happier about it than you are. But I seem to be stuck here for the time being. I've got no idea how to get home, and going off on my own in this unfamiliar time period isn't such a grand idea, either. Especially now that you've opened your big mouth and 'married' us. So for the sake of this make-believe union, can't we please just try to get along?"

He stared at me for a count of three. Finally, a reluctant grin lifted one corner of his mouth.

"Looks like we're stuck with each other, doesn't it. Neither one of us has much of a choice."

It wasn't what I would call a warm welcome. But it was *something*. One small step toward getting along. At least until we could figure out a way to get me swooshed back to my own era.

Chapter 5
RACHEL

Word of our purported nuptials must have spread through the tight-knit Glenbrook community at the speed of light. About midnight, a horrible racket outside awakened me. A cacophony of banging pots and pans. Jangling bells. Laughter and singing. Fists pounding on the door. Stomping of boots.

"That son of a –" Lucas threw back the folds of his pallet and leaped to his feet, hastily jamming one leg after the other into his trousers.

"What's going on? What is it?" Clutching the blankets to my chest, I sat up in bed.

"Sounds like they've decided to give us a shivaree." It was a growl.

"A shiv-a-*what*?"

"Shivaree." He was already shrugging his arms into a shirt, fingers fumbling with the buttons. "A welcome-home for newlyweds. Half celebration and half sheer annoyance."

I still didn't get it.

"To embarrass us," he spit out. "To interrupt. . . *er*, whatever we *might* have been doing."

He bent to peer out the window.

"How many are out there?"

The moonlight was enough to show me his grimace. "Two dozen or so by the look of it."

Through the window I could make out lanterns swaying in the dark, bodies moving. The outrageous racket continued.

"How embarrassing!"

"Exactly what they intend." Despite himself, his grimace was softening. I suspected he was fighting a full-on grin.

I eyed the swirl of bodies outside, moving in the lamplight. "So, now what?"

"Now we go out and greet them, pass around a few bottles of whiskey, and hope they have enough grace to go home very soon." He stepped away from the window. "Better put your clothes on."

Lucas turned his back and began folding the blankets of his pallet. His way of granting me privacy, I presumed. Slipping out of bed, I reached for one of the dresses he'd brought me yesterday and slid it over my head. Luckily, the size *had* been right. My fingers fumbled with the unfamiliar buttons, then flew as I attempted a quick braid.

The noise had only intensified by the time Lucas finally threw open the door. There on the doorstep stood a laughing, playful horde - young and old, men and women, breaths rising in frosty plumes in the cold. Pushing and elbowing each other, they crowded through the doorway and into the cabin, eagerly embracing its warmth.

Soon the room was packed. The first wave made themselves at home by perching on the bed, settling on the hearth, and commandeering the cabin's only two chairs. As others straggled in it became standing room only. The minstrels in the group struck up song after song, their off-key enthusiasm enhanced by bottles being passed around. Lucas swept two bottles off his shelf to add to the libations, but the whiskey was in no danger of running out; the crowd had brought a goodly supply along with them.

Men slapped Lucas heartily on the back, teasing him good-naturedly about succumbing to the chains of matrimony. Meanwhile the women clustered around me, all smiles and polite getting-to-know-you questions.

I couldn't help but laugh, watching the scene unfold. Across the room, Lucas remained visible in the sea of humanity. He stood at least half a head taller than the other men, for one thing. The glimmer of a smile softened his face, and I noticed his ears were turning red. All in all, he seemed to be doing a grand job of keeping up the charade of being a newlywed.

I couldn't help but wonder what it might be like to launch a married life for real with this giant of a man. With neighbors who so obviously loved and respected him.

But no, I chided myself quickly. It was a lovely fantasy – the warmth, the feeling of togetherness, of belonging. In reality, though, I *didn't* belong. Not in this place. Not in this *time.* Lucas was a pretty good actor. But he didn't truly belong to me.

My job – my *only* job – was to get back to my own time as quickly as possible. To my sister, who needed me. To the life that, troubled though it was, was *my* life. I hated to think what additional trouble Serena might have manufactured while I was gone. Yes, my focus needed to remain on finding answers to my time-travel dilemma. *Fast.*

There was no clock in Lucas' cabin. But by the time the last reveler finally staggered through the door, I figured it had to be somewhere around 2 a.m.

"Thank heavens they're gone!" Exhausted, I flopped back on the bed as Lucas shut the door. I craned my head to look at him. "Do they do that for *every* newly-married couple?"

He turned that annoyingly charming smile on me. "Only the ones they like."

I resisted the urge to stick out my tongue. "I'd hate to see what they do to ones they *don't* like!"

He laughed heartily, as if I'd finally reached his funny bone. A sound that made me wish I could hear him laugh like that for, oh, about a dozen years. Then he sobered. "Unfortunately, they won't be very pleased if they ever find out we aren't really married."

Turning on my side, I propped myself on one elbow. "Don't tell me they would show up with a shotgun and a preacher and try to make it official."

He grinned. "That's a bridge I hope we don't ever need to cross. So, please. If I have to beg, I'll beg. Help me keep up appearances until we figure out how to get you back where you belong, or I'll never hear the end of this."

"Fine. But then how exactly do you plan to explain your 'wife's' sudden disappearance?"

His lips thinned. "I'll think of something. I'll just say you ran off, maybe." My raised eyebrow must have made him think. "Women do that, you know."

There was a trace of something in his voice - something raw and deep and vulnerable. Pain. But it was quickly gone.

"All right. You must be tired after all that. Let's get some sleep." Without waiting for agreement, he began padding around the cabin, snuffing out the candles one by one.

When the room was dark, I shucked off my dress and collapsed back on the bed, wrapping myself in the soothing weight of the blankets.

I *was* tired. But they'd been nice folks, I thought as I stared up into the darkness. Friendly. Welcoming. A good-hearted bunch. I'd enjoyed them all. Could even see myself becoming friends with the women I'd met, if things were different.

I hadn't exactly leveled with them, which made me feel slightly guilty. I had wangled myself into their midst, but my presence here was grounded in a lie. Hardly the way to launch a real friendship. How would they feel later, when Lucas made excuses to cover my absence?

Sure, I was eager to get home. But something deep in my belly rebelled at the notion he was planning to tell his friends and neighbors I'd run off.

Chapter 6

RACHEL

Two days dragged slowly by. According to the calendar tacked to Lucas' wall, that made today February 11th. TGI Friday, right? Not that the weekend ahead would bring much of a change, I supposed.

Tired of staying home reading by the woodstove while Lucas took care of his timber business, I finally begged to come with him. I was curious. I was bored.

He grimaced but surprisingly didn't object.

The air felt bitter cold against my face as we stepped outside, but at least the skiff of snow around the cabin had finally melted. Lucas had bundled me up in one of his old coats, big enough to swamp me. It smelled like him, I thought as I turned up the collar and snugged the top button. Woodsy, spicy. An oddly reassuring scent.

The tails of the coat hung to my ankles, hardly a fashion statement. But between that and the heavy skirt, at least my legs would stay warm.

I jammed my hands deep in the coat pockets we began to walk, side by side, toward the dock at Glenbrook. The vista ahead was oddly familiar - the lake, the humps of distant mountains, a widening sweep of meadow as we drew closer. But my eyes kept drifting to the surrounding hills, shockingly denuded of timber.

I'd read about it, of course. The Comstock mines had jokingly been dubbed the "graveyard" of Tahoe's forests, thanks to their voracious appetite for timber. But seeing nothing but stumps all around me made my stomach knot. It would be another century before second-growth trees would begin to resemble the old-growth, and even then the forests would never be the same.

"What's the population here?"

"At Glenbrook, you mean?" Lucas angled his head toward me, not breaking stride. "About two hundred, I guess."

I nodded. "That would explain why I'm not seeing many houses."

His voice turned sharp. "Not many?" He might as well have been asking what was wrong with my eyesight.

Ah. To him, the dozen or so homes we'd passed counted as a thriving settlement.

I wasn't about to describe what Tahoe would look like 130 years from now. He probably wouldn't believe it. Instead, I changed the subject. "What's that over there?"

His eyes followed my finger. "The building belching smoke? That's Pray's sawmill. The earliest mill at Glenbrook, built back in '63. Captain Pray also owns the *Governor Blasdel*. You'll see her as we get closer. A 42-foot paddlewheeler," he tacked on, seeing the confusion on my face. "Built to tow logs across the lake to his mill."

Warming to his subject, Lucas turned tour guide. "And those smaller puffs of smoke you see off to the north? Those are the three newer mills. Carson & Tahoe Lumber built the first one in '73 and a second in '75. Then there's an even-newer mill at Crystal Bay, built about eight years ago for Sierra Nevada Wood & Lumber."

"That's a lot of lumber mills!"

Lucas just grinned. "There's a lot of timber to be worked. Or at least there was."

I glanced around again at the stumps. "Yeah, I can see that. Looks like most of it's gone already."

His face shuttered. I'd hit on a sore subject, apparently. "That's true enough, here. But there's plenty of logging still going on at the south end of the lake and into Lake Valley."

"I bet it really used to be pretty." I couldn't keep the wistfulness from my voice.

It was Lucas' turn to change the subject. By the time the long wooden dock at Glenbrook came into view, he'd given me a thumbnail sketch of D.L. Bliss's lumbering operation, pointing out his vast network of railroads, flumes, and mills. Over the previous twelve years, Bliss had assembled an empire indeed.

A narrow-gauge railroad ferried flatcars of timber from the sawmill at Glenbrook to the top of Spooner Summit to the east. At the 7, 146-foot summit, the wood was transferred to a 12-mile V-flume and sent careening down the mountainside to the V&T Railroad yards at Carson City. Bliss had embraced the latest technology: three powerful Baldwin locomotives to pull the flatcars of his Lake Tahoe Railroad. And that magical new invention, the telephone, to coordinate operation. A dedicated stretch of wire linked Glenbrook with Carson City – one of the first phone systems in the West.

Lucas' operation was hardly on the same scale as Bliss. But he'd been building his own small lumber business for five years, he told me. Acquiring land; even purchasing a steamship to ferry floating timbers to a mill.

Beyond those brief admissions, he didn't dish too many details. If I had to guess, he wasn't exactly pleased with his success so far. There was a tension about him, a way of cutting off his words as we drew closer to the water's edge. As if he didn't want me asking too many questions about the way things were going. Either that, or he was hiding something.

I was polite enough not to pry. Knowing Lucas, further questions probably wouldn't have dislodged any further useful information, anyway.

As we stepped out on the heavy wooden dock, Lucas gestured to a large steamer tethered at the far end. "That one's mine - the *Meteor*," he said. "Well, mine and the bank's."

The *Meteor* proved to be paddlewheeler with a swooping iron hull, prominent raked smokestack, covered aft, and tall, jutting pilot house. Seventy-five feet long, she was roomy enough to accommodate dozens of passengers and sturdy enough to survive whatever weather tantrums Lake Tahoe might throw her way.

A narrow wooden gangplank with ropes at the sides for handrails angled from the dock to the ship. Leading the way, Lucas extended a hand to steady me. I seized it tightly, grateful for the reassuring pressure of his fingers. Between my long skirts and his heavy coat around my shoulders, I felt much less than agile. The cleated gangplank rocked slightly as I took my first step. The last thing I needed was to trip over one of the narrow cleats and wind up in Tahoe's icy waters wearing all these clothes!

Once both feet were planted firmly on the *Meteor*'s solid deck, I exhaled in relief. A flurry of activity surrounded me. Lucas quickly disappeared on some errand as I stayed by the rail, trying to stay out of the way. Deckhands scurried this way and that. The gangplank was raised and hauled aboard, and before I knew it, a whistle blew and we were under way and heading south, a dark column of smoke belching from the tall, raked smokestack.

Our destination, Lucas had explained, was a spot on Tahoe's South shore called Rowland's. It took me a few minutes to realize it must be the spot I knew as Al Tahoe. But as we pulled in sight of the shore two hours later, the scene resembled nothing familiar.

Just as at Glenbrook, a long, heavy-timbered dock greeted us. An *extremely* long dock, this time, as the water near the shore was too shallow for ships. But in place of the swath of homes and businesses lining the lake in my time, here a sweep of rails cut the largely empty horizon. According to Lucas this was the Lake Valley Railroad, acquired from logger George Chubbuck just a year earlier to enhance Bliss's Carson & Tahoe Lumber operation. Chubbuck himself was evidently still around. Joining me at the rail Lucas pointed farther south and, with a hand over one eye, I could just make out Chubbuck's logging camp in the distance, all tall piles of logs and men scampering about like ants.

Bliss himself was now the proud owner of more than ten thousand acres here at the south end of the Lake. Lucas hardly rivaled that figure but, to my ears, his timber acreage was still astonishing: a thousand wooded acres that stretched south into Lake Valley. Probably near what I called Meyers.

After the *Meteor*'s lines were made fast to the pier and the gangplank again extended, Lucas again appeared at my side.

"The docks can be a dangerous place for visitors. Too many heavy wagons, as you can see, and loads that can shift at any time. I won't be long. Better you just stay aboard." I heard a hint of question in his voice. He wanted my cooperation, but wasn't going to order me to stay.

"That's fine. The pilot house will probably give me a better view, anyway."

I was right. Once I'd clambered up the metal stairs - not an easy feat, as my heels kept tangling in my long skirt - the windows of the pilot house offered a crow's-eye view of the bustling activity on shore. I watched in amazement as giant logs were dumped from flatcars into the water, then corralled with ropes to create a massive, floating raft. The entire process took several hours but was quicker than I would have expected for such heavy work. By noon we were ready to push off again and begin our slow return, towing the giant raft of logs behind us.

I heard Lucas' boots clang on the metal decking before I felt his presence behind me. He stood so close I caught a whiff of the pungent shaving soap he'd used this morning.

"Enjoying yourself?" It was a chuckle.

I turned to look in those blue eyes, and for a second I was floating, losing myself in their depths.

I caught myself. "Actually, yes! It's been fun to watch!"

He chuckled again and, reaching up, pushed a wind-whipped strand of hair behind my ear. As if suddenly realizing he'd unconsciously crossed a line, he took a step back.

I instantly missed his closeness. *Why?*

Embarrassed, I turned my back to him and stared out over the water, trying to collect my thoughts. When I turned around again, he was gone. My eyes swung around, searching.

He'd evidently decided to relieve the helmsman, as there he stood at the wheel, legs braced, hauling on the tall wooden spokes to swing the ship's nose gently into Lake Tahoe's swells. Behind us, the raft of logs trailed like an obedient flock of sheep following their shepherd.

Another harvest that had denuded one more swath of once-virgin land, but also much-needed income for Lucas.

Part of me wanted to ask him more about the current state of the timber business. Operators large and small seemed to be pushing farther and farther afield in the quest for the living raw material required to keep the Comstock humming. But it was a zero-sum game, wasn't it? Eventually they would run out of forests to cut.

And if my somewhat hazy memory of Comstock history was correct, the mines of Virginia City had already begun slowing as silver ore petered out. Was timber really the right business to be in? Or was Lucas simply hoping a larger operator like Bliss would buy him out, allowing him to move on to fresh pursuits and new horizons?

But there was no further opportunity to talk, even once the *Meteor* docked back at Glenbrook several hours later. Here, at least, I was encouraged to leave the ship while the logging crews worked. "Just don't go too far," Lucas admonished. "I'll walk home with you when we're finished here."

And so I sat on the rough wooden dock, legs dangling over the edge, arms braced behind me. As I watched, the shore crew hoisted the logs from their watery cradle onto flatcars for their journey up the narrow-gauge to Spooner. The bodies of the crew moved in a well-choreographed rhythm born of long experience. Lucas moved among them, pointing and cajoling, bending to lend a hand here and adding a well-timed thrust of his shoulder there.

Once again, he was clearly in his element. Something about his competence with ship, logs, and crew brought a swell of warmth to my belly.

Suddenly a well-polished shoe appeared beside my hand on the rough wooden dock. Raising the other hand to shield my eyes from the sun, I looked up.

A man in a dark grey wool suit loomed over me. Greasy salt-and-pepper curls spilled over his collar. The knees of his trousers bagged slightly and the suit could have used a good pressing, but its details spoke of money: carefully-matched seams and neat edge-stitching, the hallmarks of an expensive San Francisco tailor. His boots, though scuffed on the toes, appeared to be fine leather. His hands were braced atop a gold-headed cane.

The man touched the brim of his hat briefly, lips tipped up in an imitation of a smile.

"Ah, so it's true! I heard my friend Lucas got himself married. You must be the new Mrs. Russell."

I wasn't quite sure how to respond. For a 'friend' of Lucas's, he hardly seemed friendly. I limited myself to a small nod of acknowledgment.

Steely eyes raked me from head to dangling feet as the fake smile disappeared. "Please remind him he has a debt to repay, and he's already in arrears on interest. June 30th the full principal comes due. And that's exactly how long I'm willing to wait. No longer."

Smug. That was the feeling he gave off as he turned on one booted heel and strode casually back toward the shore.

So, Lucas owed money to this awful man? My stomach twisted. And he not only owed money, the loan was delinquent?

There was something especially disconcerting about the man's final words. It hadn't been a threat, exactly, it was – *gloating*. June 30th was the deadline. And he didn't expect Lucas to pay. What exactly did that mean? What collateral would he be losing? The pinch in my belly tightened. Had Lucas mortgaged his cabin? His interest in the ship? Both??

Somehow this new information surprised me. Lucas was such a hard worker. So good at his trade. So effective at piloting the ship and maneuvering logs. So capable around his men. Why hadn't he mentioned a financial disaster looming?

Well, he hadn't confided *much* to me about himself or his life, after all. Sure, he'd showed me the *Meteor* and explained a little about timber. Pointed out the railroad and how the logs made their way from forest to the mines. But he'd shared little that was personal. Nothing to explain those letters I'd found bound up in a ribbon, for instance.

Then again, why *should* he confide in me? I was just a temporary nuisance in his life. One he hoped would be gone soon.

From the corner of my eye I saw the arrogant little man had stopped at the edge of the dock. He stood casually, half-turned toward the ship, as if studying the water. Or perhaps he was studying the *Meteor* as she bobbed against her moorings. Far enough away I couldn't see his eyes. Still too close for comfort.

"That guy's got all the warm-and-fuzzies of a flippin' Charles Manson," I gritted to myself.

A chuckle made me turn. A young woman stood behind me, clad in a long blue gown, two small girls at her side. I flushed. I hadn't noticed her approach. I'd been too distracted by that awful man.

The woman's bright blue eyes seemed to twinkle with warmth. Eyes that now drilled into my own, as if she were searching, searching. . . then she nodded, evidently satisfied by what she'd found.

"I couldn't help overhearing." That happy chuckle erupted again.

Blood rushed to my face. "Sorry, just a figure of speech. Don't mind me," I hedged, shooting her an answering grin in hopes she wouldn't press any further.

"I understand." She bent to kiss the little girls, then shooed them off to the beach to play, with firm instructions to remain within sight.

"My name's Charity," she said, extending one slim hand. "Charity Danforth. And you are -?"

"Rachel Moretti." My ears were still burning with embarrassment but I shook, pleased to find a good, firm shake in return.

She was a pretty woman. Blonde with a touch of red; hair that sparkled in the late afternoon sun. Eyes the color of the serene Tahoe waves, a deep green-grey. A good woman, a strong woman, was my first impression. Also nobody to mess with.

"*I understand*," she'd said just a moment ago. What exactly did she mean? Just how much did she understand?

"So, when are you from?" she asked.

Not *where* are you from. That disarming smile pinned me.

"What's that?"

She waved a palm airily, her smile spreading wider. "Oh, I think you know exactly what I said! Come." She settled on the rough wooden dock beside me, legs dangling like mine, paying no mind to any risk to her pretty blue skirt. "I haven't seen you around here before. You a new arrival?"

"Just got here a few days ago." That part, at least, was true.

In the distance, I saw the older man reach the end of the dock and turn around. He glared back at us before finally stepping off the dock and striding away.

Thank goodness he was gone. Something about him gave me chills.

"So, tell me. When *are* you from?" Charity insisted. "What year?"

My jaw dropped. When I finally managed to gather my wits about me, we talked. And talked. And *talked.*

Charity, it turned out, was no stranger to time-travel, having unwittingly made a time-leap herself two years ago. In her case, she'd gone from a modern-day tour of the historic Danforth mansion to finding herself in that very same parlor in Victorian times, face-to-face with rancher Josiah Danforth in the flesh.

"It was quite a shock," she laughed merrily. I could only grin in agreement.

Like me, at first she'd only been anxious to figure out how the magic had happened and how to get back. "Except fate stepped in and had something to say about the whole thing, too," she chuckled. "I fell in love with Josiah. And finally I realized that this time is where I truly belong after all."

The glow in her cheeks testified it had been the right decision.

The common elements in both our stories were a full moon and some kind of electrical energy or flash of bright light. There'd been a talisman of sorts for both of us, too – for her, it was a photo of Josiah encased in a silver picture frame that (as nearly as she could tell) had launched her back to his time. For me it had been the crystal pendant, which somehow had channeled the raw power of the lightning storm.

But exactly how I could harness those disparate elements to propel myself back where I belonged remained a mystery.

"Heaven only knows what's happened while I've been gone." My voice held the ragged edge of worry. I told her about Serena, my know-it-all seventeen-year-old sister, and the new boyfriend enticing her down a dangerous path.

As we talked, Charity's eyes flicked repeatedly to her two step-daughters on the shoreline, like a mama bear, watching her cubs. It was far too cold for them to take off their shoes and stick toes in the frigid water, but they were running and laughing, amusing themselves by throwing rocks in the water. The gentle smile on Charity's face testified she loved her step-daughters dearly. So she understood a caretaker's worry. It was a relief to spilly my own worries to such a kind listening ear.

"It's been three days since I got here. But has the same length of time elapsed for Serena? Is she tearing her hair out, wondering where I am? Or when I finally get back, will I discover no time at all has elapsed, because the future hasn't happened yet?" My fingers twisted anxiously in the edge of my coat.

Charity's eyebrows drew together. "That's a really good question, and I confess I don't know the answer. But as for getting back, you can certainly *try* as soon as next month's full moon. Nothing's guaranteed, I'm afraid."

Charity explained that she herself had tried several times to make the reverse time-leap—unsuccessfully, she confided, before resolving to remain with Josiah and his girls. "I do think all the details have to be lined up as closely as possible to the way they were when you arrived," she continued. "Your best chance is probably near a solstice or some other big celestial event, not just an ordinary full moon. It was the full moon closest to the summer Solstice that triggered my arrival. We're not the only ones this has happened to, you know. One man I met was able to engineer his own reverse time trip when the Winter Solstice enhanced the full moon's power."

That, at least, cleared up a bit of the mystery: it had taken the giant Snow Moon plus the added zip of the electrical storm to propel Lucas into the future, then carry both of us back here.

Oddly enough, for Charity the solution hadn't been returning at all. Instead, when the time came, Charity had decided to stay in the Victorian era with the love of her life. That was something I'd never even considered. "When you finally meet the right one, you just know what to do," she smiled.

The right one. The love of one's life. Why did Lucas' face pop into my mind when I heard that?

Reaching down, Charity squeezed my hand where it rested on the dock. "You still have plenty of time to plan. Pull out an almanac and see what moon phase might work best. And if there's anything I can do to help you get ready. . ."

I squeezed her fingers back. "You've already been an immense help! I can't thank you enough. Just knowing I'm not alone here is amazing."

I'd found a friend.

I could hardly wait to tell Lucas what I'd learned about getting home again, uncertain though the timing was. And I needed to tell him about my uncomfortable encounter with the irritating man on the dock, too.

But back at the cabin that evening, Lucas' reaction wasn't what I'd expected. Instead of excitement, he'd greeted the news about Charity and her views on celestial mechanics with a dismissive wave. And when I mentioned the banker – for Lucas confirmed it was banker Sylvester Sullivan who approached me – his face had merely darkened.

"Unfortunately, I trusted the man once," Lucas conceded, his jaw tightening. "But it's not really your problem, is it."

That's all he would say. His voice wasn't just angry, but defensive. And once again, that got me wondering what he might be hiding.

While our dinner stew simmered on the cookstove, Lucas allowed me to unwrap and inspect his injured hand. The poultice had done its job. After only two days, the wound was healing around the margins. When I commented on how well it looked, though, his brow simply furrowed.

"What exactly has got you all riled up?" I huffed, settling back on my heels. "Worried that something might actually be going *right* for a change?"

He exhaled sharply and his eyes slid away from mine. *Bingo.* I'd hit home. I'd been right about the healing salve, and somehow that irritated him, too. Someone with knowledge that proved helpful? That got his back up, simply because it hadn't been his idea?!

His eyes found mine again. "Sorry. I know I'm being difficult. I owe you a debt of gratitude for that foul-smelling concoction. It does seem to be working." His jaw tightened.

The apology had been grudging. But it had been an apology, nonetheless.

After cleaning the wound and applying a fresh poultice, I rewrapped his hand carefully with a fresh rag and tied the ends tight. Brushing my palms against my skirt, I stood.

"Another few days and we can probably do without the bandage." I managed a smile.

He nodded. A change of subject seemed in order.

"Do you happen to own an almanac?" I'd already explained the role a solstice might play in my potential return journey.

His relaxed, charming smile was back. "You bet. We'll pull it out after supper and try to figure out what might be the best time to send you on your way."

A leaden weight settled in the pit of my stomach. Why was sending me home the first topic about which Lucas sounded truly enthusiastic? I was eager, too. But his attitude stung, somehow.

Soon the stew was ready, and we settled into what had become our usual spots at the kitchen table. But as warm and hearty as the food was, the conversation quickly turned chilly. I made the mistake of expressing my dismay over Tahoe's old growth disappearing. "Sure, some of the trees will grow back eventually, but that virgin forest - once it's gone, it's gone forever," I mused.

"It's not just my livelihood," Lucas bristled. "Those trees mean wages for hundreds of hard-working men from woodchoppers to the boys on the railroad. And they're the lifeblood of the Virginia mines. Which employ thousands more." His voice darkened. "You're starting to sound like that pantywaist Bliss, who insists his workmen spare any tree less than fifteen inches in diameter."

"Well, I happen to think that's a grand idea!" I retorted. "The forest is still being sacrificed, but at least it leaves hope for regrowth!"

The set of his jaw told me continuing this discussion was fruitless. I cleared away the supper dishes, then tried to lower the temperature between us.

"Maybe now would be a good time to take a look at that almanac."

"It's late. We can do it in the morning."

My heart sank. "It'll only take a few minutes to finish the dishes. Let's go through the almanac afterward. Please."

Lucas looked ready to argue, then grimly set his mouth. "Whatever you say."

I had pushed for what I wanted, and that, too irritated him. Lucas clearly wasn't used to women setting their own agenda.

But I could feel desperation creeping in. I needed to get back to my sister. To get back to a life that was familiar. To leave Lucas to stew in his own unhappiness.

Once the dishes were washed and put away, Lucas was true to his word. He pulled out a slim paperback volume from his bookshelf and showed me how to read the lunar tables.

"See here, next month's full moon is March 9," he said, pointing to a small round icon on the chart. "But if what Charity said is accurate, your best chance of making a time leap work is probably here, on the full moon closest to the summer solstice." His forefinger tapped another line on the page.

June 5th. Four full months away.

My heart dropped. A terribly long time to wait. And who knew if I'd be successful even then?

He closed the almanac and returned it to its spot on the shelf without another word. I'd gotten what I'd wanted: answers about the coming solstice. The grim set of his mouth said he was as unhappy as I was about what it meant.

That night after all the lamps were snuffed out, I tossed and turned on Lucas' narrow bed. I was yearning to embrace Serena, to make sure she was okay. Anxious to pick up a daily routine that felt normal again. To wear my own clothes. Pursue my own dreams, humble though they were right at the moment. I'd even be tempted to throw my arms around prickly

Devon Williams if I saw him. And yes, it would be a happy day to leave this cold, distant man far, far behind me.

Lucas's unyielding reserve was painful to be around, even though I knew it probably stemmed from being badly hurt somehow. But he wasn't just concealing emotions from me; he was hiding something else, too. Instinct told me it was something bigger than just a delinquent loan. There was some other painful secret he was holding close, though I couldn't imagine what it might be. Lucas' outer shell was as hard as those old-growth trees; no way was he going to allow me to drill in far enough to discover what really had gone wrong in his life.

I flopped to my other side, throwing an arm over my eyes and wishing for sleep that failed to come.

So why did Lucas' secret bother me? Well, because I was a 'fixer' by nature. The person with answers for everyone else. Solutions to make things go more smoothly at work. Options to help Serena navigate the rapids of teenage angst. I enjoyed being the one who came up with great ideas. For everyone except myself, of course. I hadn't quite managed to fix my *own* life.

My much-anticipated career in medicine, for example, didn't look like it would ever happen. Doctoring Lucas's hand was probably the closest I'd come to giving medical care. And, to be honest, it made me sad that I'd never found a "love of my life" like Charity. That solution, too, had eluded me.

I'd tried all the usual safe avenues: friends of friends. Even a dating app once or twice. Survived a few boring evenings. Met a few nice men. Nobody who made my heart race, though. Not like it did with – I stopped myself before finishing the thought.

Everything was just so strange and different. Back in my own time I'd had the catering gig. It wasn't much, but it was honest work that paid the bills. A routine that was comfortable. And I did enjoy cooking, at least when Devon wasn't breathing down my neck. Most of all, I'd had my sister.

But here? Here I was nobody. Just a burr under Lucas's saddle. An annoyance to be tolerated until we could figure out the magic that would set us both free. I had no job, no purpose, other than maintaining my fictitious role as Lucas' wife.

A wet nose nudged my hand, and a weight settled against my side. As if he'd been reading my mind, Hasty settled his big head on my shoulder. What a sweet dog. I wrapped an arm around his neck, pressing my forehead into his warm fur.

A dull *whump-whump* sounded from across the room. Lucas was pounding his pillow. He hadn't been able to fall asleep, either, apparently.

I didn't need any further reminders. I was *in his space*, and he was getting understandably grumpy about it. He hadn't complained yet about sleeping on the floor, but that pallet certainly didn't look comfortable.

It was hard to tell who was more eager for me to leave so life could return to normal, me or Lucas.

Chapter 7
LUCAS

It was the second of March and the day had dawned clear and cold. But the bitterest cold, had vanished. Already, I could feel the days getting longer.

I'd spent the morning tromping the hills behind the cabin with my rifle, hoping to replenish our meat supply. I'd been in luck; two limp rabbits lay beside the stump I used as a butchering block. None too fat, either of them; it had been a long, harsh winter. But they'd make a welcome addition to the stew pot this evening.

I was just skinning out the second one when Rachel rounded the corner of the cabin, a basket of wet laundry on one hip. Her eyes flicked to the knife in my hand, then surveyed the bloody stump.

"Don't let me stop you." I gestured toward the empty clothesline strung between two trees. "Though it's still a mite cold for wash to dry, don't you think?"

Rachel plunked the basket on the ground and crossed her arms over her chest. "It's already warming up. By this afternoon it'll be well above freezing. Why do you second-guess everything I do?"

I took a minute to consider her jab. Was she right? Was I second-guessing? I harrumphed just to let her know I'd heard her and that my answering silence was deliberate, then returned to skinning the rabbit.

Out of the corner of my eye, I couldn't help noticing she made an appealing sight, even with that scowl turned in my direction. Charity had paid us a visit earlier in the week, delivering a few more things for Rachel to wear, and I had to admit she looked pretty darn fine in the dress she had on today. Fitted tightly in the bodice, it showed off her figure to a fare-thee-well. Not that Rachel seemed aware of how appealing she looked. Which only added to the attraction.

My knife slipped unexpectedly, almost nicking my finger. I would do well to pay closer attention to my work and less to that dress, I reminded myself sternly. Besides, the last thing I needed was to warm up to another female. Rachel was an unasked-for millstone about my neck. End of story.

A faint noise made me glance up again. Standing closer now, Rachel had gone pale, eyes on the pile of entrails.

"What's wrong? Haven't you ever seen rabbit guts before?"

She shook her head sharply, a quick no, before backing up several steps. Snatching up the laundry basket again, she turned. "I'll finish hanging the wash later."

"What, did you think meat just shows up magically on the dinner table?" I called to her retreating back.

That did it. Angry now, she dropped the laundry basket to the ground and swung about to face me. Her hands found her hips again. Unfortunately, the movement stretched the cloth of her dress even more tightly across her bosom, prompting a sudden unwanted answering tightening in my trousers.

"The local fish you've caught have been awesome, and the dried venison you cooked up a few days ago wasn't bad. But I'm sorry." She pointed to the bloody stump. "Skinning a rabbit is just plain gross. And no, I haven't been treated to a view of rabbit guts before."

I lowered my eyes to my work with the knife, hoping she'd take the hint and leave. "So don't watch, then."

Behind me I heard the scrape of the basket as she hoisted it from the ground, but I didn't turn to watch her departure. I finished skinning out the second rabbit, then neatly butchered the two carcasses, throwing chunks of meat into the metal pot I'd brought with me. I'd take the skin, bones and entrails up into the forest later to dispose of them far away from the cabin. The bears were still asleep, but no need to encourage cats or coyotes to hang around.

For some reason, our testy exchange bothered me, though. I found myself mulling it over as I cleaned my knife and my hands at the pump, wondering if I should have curbed my tongue and not been quite so sharp. Rachel had tried her best to make herself useful while she was here. She'd taken over more and more of the cooking, a task she seemed to enjoy. More than once, I'd caught her humming softly to herself over the stove. And truth be told, she was a far better cook than I could ever hope to be. That, at least, had been a happy surprise.

I grabbed the pot of raw meat and returned to the cabin, letting the front door slam behind me. But her attitude about the rabbit annoyed me. I was doing my best to keep food on our table. And she somehow found it disgusting?! It was a slap in the face.

Rachel was peeling an onion when I walked in. I set the metal pot on the chopping block beside her. "Stew meat, if you want it."

She didn't look up.

I folded my arms across my chest and moved closer.

"Look. We've got only one more week together, assuming that the full moon works its magic March 9th. And that's best case. Worst case, it's three months 'til the solstice in June. Either way, somehow or other we have to figure out a way to get along in the meantime."

Rachel's knife made angry rhythmic clicks as she diced the onion. "That magic day can't come any too soon for me. I can't wait to get back to normal!"

Frustrated, I threw both hands in the air. *She* was having a hard time being here?! I was every bit as eager as she was to return to "normal"!

I was about to mutter words I would probably regret about prissy females and ungrateful guests when a knock sounded at the door. Grateful for the interruption, I strode to the front door and threw it open.

Some days, it seemed, my luck could only get worse. There on my front doorstep was Sullivan.

"What do you want?"

Sullivan merely grinned, a smirk that didn't reach his eyes. Peering over my shoulder at Rachel, he lifted an eyebrow. "Like I told your *wife*," he began, emphasizing the final word. "Time is running out." His eyes returned to me again. "Not sure whether she passed along the message."

Rachel quietly moved up to stand beside me, wiping her hands on her apron. We were no longer at odds, I noticed.

In some strange way, Sullivan's presence had forged us into a team, standing tall against a common enemy.

"I passed along the message," she replied coolly. "You don't need to repeat it."

Sullivan touched two fingers to his hat brim. "I won't belabor the point any further then. Like I said, you've got 'til June 30th. Not a day longer."

He hesitated then, eyes raking the cabin's interior as if taking inventory of the contents. Everything inside would soon be his, if he had his way. A prospect that looked more and more likely with each passing day.

"Till I see you again, then." At last he gave a short nod and turned away.

This time I made sure the slam of the cabin door could likely be heard halfway across the lake. "The bastard," I growled, sinking down at the table. "That arrogant, insufferable bastard. He just came to gloat!"

I lowered my head to my hands.

I had fought and clawed, worked and sweat. Only to still find myself teetering on the verge of losing everything.

June 30th. Less than four months away. Sullivan already knew I wouldn't make it. He was rubbing it in.

I heard the swish of fabric and the dull scratch of a chair leg as Rachel took the seat beside me.

"Lucas." A hand settled softly on my forearm. "Lucas, what's the matter."

I raised my head, ignoring the tears stinging my eyes. "Nothing that I shouldn't have realized a long time ago. I'm a fool when it comes to business. My brother always said I should've taken the safe way, the slow way, like he did. 'Buy some cattle. Stay away from mining and timber,' he kept saying. I should've listened."

"So you didn't do things *his* way." Her voice was soft, reassuring. "That doesn't mean what you did was wrong."

I laughed, a sad and awkward sound. "Oh, he was definitely right and I was definitely wrong." I rose from the table, turning my back to her. "He may be my younger brother, but that's how it's been all our lives. He always wins. And I always lose."

The chair scraped again and I felt that soft hand descend on my shoulder. I shook it off, spinning to face her.

"I don't need your sympathy."

Tears filled her eyes, and I suddenly felt like a cad. She'd been trying to help. I knew that. Still, I couldn't seem to stop myself. Pushing her away felt right. It felt *necessary.*

"Please, Lucas. Let's talk about it."

Striding to the door, I yanked it open and strode through. Hasty slipped through behind me just before the door closed behind me. I hadn't stopped to grab my mackinaw. I didn't really care.

I knew I was being unfair. Rachel *was* only trying to help. But I wasn't ready to confide in anyone. It wouldn't do any good. Besides, with any luck she'd soon be gone, anyway.

My feet beat a dull rhythm on the cold, hard ground as I strode toward the beach. My breath came in spurts. Hasty effortlessly matched my pace.

Catapulting Rachel back to her own time couldn't happen soon enough for me. She would be so much happier. And I'd have my cabin to myself again. Me and Hasty. The dog brushed against my legs, as if reading my thoughts.

I'd have my dog, my cabin, my life to myself again. At least until June 30th, when all bets were off. But a huge relief in the meantime, at least.

Except – except *I* knew I was lying to myself.

Rachel had been the one good thing that had happened to me lately. Weird though the circumstances had been that brought us together, I'd begun looking forward to seeing her at the end of the day. Enjoyed having someone else in the cabin, even when we didn't talk.

Difficult as it had been for me to adjust, it must have been a hundred times more difficult for her, suddenly finding herself in a foreign world. Yet she hadn't complained.

I kicked myself, suddenly realizing I'd never asked how she felt. It had to be frightening, disconcerting, even terrifying to be swept away like that. I knew she was worried about her sister. But she must also be wondering if she'd make it home again, ever.

Yet for the most part, Rachel had stayed determinedly cheerful. She'd done her best to make herself useful. And her cooking?! I gave a wry chuckle. I had no idea how she did it with my limited supplies, but she'd definitely been a blessing on the culinary front.

Slowing my pace, I stroked Hasty's head absently, then turned around and aimed my steps toward home again. Obediently, the dog followed.

Rachel would be waiting. Wondering where I'd gone. I owed her an apology.

I was tempted to give her far more than an apology. Part of me wanted to share the truth with her. To explain just how deeply in debt I was. To confess I had no hope of repaying

Sullivan's principal in four short months. Heck, I couldn't even make the interest payments now.

Yet even if I could persuade Rachel to stay – as some faint, traitorous part of me wished she would – it wouldn't be fair to her.

My brother was right: I'd made a righteous mess of things. I couldn't drag her into it.

I squared my shoulders before reaching the cabin. Yes, best not to say anything at all beyond a curt apology. Starting over was all that was left to me now. It would be another ten years or better before I'd have anything to offer a woman.

Chapter 8
LUCAS

Tonight was the night.

Darkness surrounded us, but the full moon had already climbed above the mountains to the east, casting shadows in our path as we passed an occasional tree or rock.

A strange, uneasy excitement gripped me. Rachel, too, seemed slightly on edge, though I could tell she was trying to hide any nervousness.

Our footfalls made little noise in the soft dirt as we walked, side by side, toward Glenbrook House, with Hasty zig-zagging between us. Occasional clinks sounded from the rucksack I'd slung over my shoulder, the sound of glass hitting glass.

A few minutes more and we'd be there. Just a few minutes more.

Today was March 9th - a full moon, and not far from the equinox, if that meant anything. I should be doing a little jig at the prospect of Rachel leaving. Somehow, though, I wasn't in a dancing mood.

On my right, Rachel was silent. She'd carefully bundled up all those strange articles of clothing she'd been wearing the night she arrived – including those curiously reflective shoes, and now clutched the bundle under her right arm. She planned to change clothes in the darkness once we got closer to the spot where we'd landed on that stormy evening last month.

Had it really only been a month? I found it hard to believe. So much had happened in that short time.

The dark outline of the inn loomed up ahead, and we left the open road to duck beneath the trees where Rachel could change clothing undetected.

"I'll just take a moment." Rachel's fingers gripped my arm. "Turn your back, would you?"

I did as she requested, pivoting to put my back to the trees and fixing my eyes firmly on the roadway we just had left. Behind me, I heard the swish of fabric, a pause, then a rustle-rustle and silence.

"All done?"

"Almost."

I turned to find her seated on a large log, tying the laces of her outlandish footgear. Her legs were once again encased in what, to me, looked like men's trousers, though she'd explained several times that women wore them too, in her world.

I liked her better in the long, graceful skirt she'd just taken off.

Standing, Rachel rolled up that skirt and her other discarded articles of clothing, clutching them tight against her chest. "Not sure if I'll ever need these again –" She stopped.

Perhaps it was hitting her the same way it was hitting me. This was a bittersweet moment. A chance for her to return to her own familiar world. And quite possibly good-bye. Wonderful yet sad at the same time.

Skirting the fallen tree, she struck off across the meadow toward the dark, angular shape that was our destination. Unlike the well-traveled road we'd just left behind, the ground here was lumpy and uneven, tufts of dead grass catching at our feet. Ground squirrels had left hills, valleys, and occasional holes studding the meadow. I was tempted to reach a hand out to steady Rachel, then thought better of it.

She was doing fine on her own. She didn't need my assistance. She didn't need - well, me.

We'd halved the distance to the inn when we came to another fallen tree. The spill of moonlight illuminated its stark white trunk, bark long since vanished. Once, it had been a monster, standing sixty or more feet tall. Tonight, however, it was a lifeless fallen soldier, stubby arms cut short, its thick trunk slowly rotting away.

To my surprise, rather than detour around the obstacle, Rachel set a foot on one of the broken limbs and a hand on its top, prepared to clamber over. This time I couldn't resist. Grabbing her about the waist I hoisted her up until her feet cleared the log, then gently swung her over.

The contact, the closeness, the smell of her was intoxicating. It all felt so damn good, I regretted it the instant my hands returned to my sides. What I *wanted* was to pull her closer yet. Bury my face in that sweet-smelling hair. Let my fingers tangle in those locks.

But. . . . My fingers clenched. I needed to push such crazy thoughts away.

Tonight was about getting Rachel home again. Or at least trying.

She'd been with me a full month, now. An awkward, wonderful month. About damn time she went home, I kept telling myself.

Yes, I'd grown more and more attracted to her over the weeks together. But more than just attracted. I'd felt a surprising warm glow in my belly when our eyes met. Found myself more eager than usual to get home after work.

But her directness could be bothersome. Rachel wasn't afraid to voice her opinion, and that was foreign to me. Women usually *deferred.* Not Rachel. She wasn't afraid to express herself, even argue. It had irritated me at first. Okay, it still irritated me. And she'd also been right sometimes. Which was even more annoying.

I found myself flexing my right hand as we walked. She'd certainly been right about how to treat that, for instance. My hand was almost completely healed. A nice scar, but no infection.

Still, her mouthiness, her directness, her sassy attitude all underscored that we weren't a good match. She came from a different century. Her old life is still there, waiting for her to get back to it. Her sister was there. The fact that we came from different worlds was all too obvious.

So, why did touching her just a moment ago feel so right? My chest itched to pull her close. To kiss the sweet mouth that was so willing to tease and challenge me.

To do it would do her a disservice, even though I believed she might well kiss me back. Rachel had her sister to worry about. There was nothing here, really, to hold her. She certainly didn't need *me.*

And that reminded me even more strongly of my own failures. Rachel might not need me. But I needed to feel like a man – that I had something to offer a woman. And right now, I didn't. The thought made me grumpier than ever.

Rachel had her own life to return to, much of which I really knew nothing about. For all that she'd been easy to talk to, she'd kept a certain cloak of reserve. Secrets she wasn't sharing.

Well, I hadn't shared the sordid details of my financial catastrophe with her, either. Not that it probably mattered, at this point. There wasn't anything to be done about it now. In a few more months, Sullivan would make off with everything I owned. Probably just as well if Rachel weren't here to see it.

As if she'd read my mind and caught me thinking about her, Rachel glanced over, turning that familiar warm smile on me. And suddenly I felt incredibly guilty.

It wasn't only the depth and breadth of my financial troubles that I hadn't shared. I hadn't levelled with her about other things, too. Like the fact that I was still engaged.

Or was I? I hadn't quite resolved that not-so-tiny detail. But I certainly *had* been engaged, up until six months ago at least, when my intended had disappeared. About the same time that logging sales started to dip and I began to realize I was in deep financial hot water indeed.

Amanda, my erstwhile fiancée, had realized it even before I had. Or at least that was the best explanation I'd been able to conjure up: that she'd run off seeking greener pastures. Perhaps she'd even made her departure *with* someone. I didn't really know.

I'd tried to puzzle out how I would feel if Amanda showed up in Glenbrook again. Conflicted, that was as close as I could come to finding a word for it. We *had* been engaged, after all. She'd never officially ended the engagement. Nor had I.

And yet here I was half a year later, pretending to be happily married to Rachel.

I'd told myself that Amanda's unexplained six-month absence spoke volumes. Even the neighbors seemed convinced it was a happy thing that I'd moved on. And so I'd kept the story of my engagement to myself.

No need to share it with Rachel now.

With any luck, Rachel would be spinning off to her own time tonight, one hundred-thirty-odd years in the future. I found myself strangely torn about that: hoping for her sake that it worked. Hoping for my own sake that it wouldn't.

We'd drawn close to the sheltering wall of the inn. As if by instinct, we gravitated toward the spot where we'd awakened on the ground.

Rachel inhaled sharply, turning to face me.

"I don't quite know what to say." Moonlight bathed her upturned face, allowing me to see the wrinkle in her brow. "I'm incredibly eager to get home again, to see my sister. But somehow I hope this isn't good-bye."

My arms went around her shoulders and I drew her into a gentle hug. And then, despite myself, I hugged her tighter. Her face turned up and mine bent down at the same instant, our lips meeting. It was the first time I had actually kissed her, though I had thought about it dozens of times.

It was a sweet, gentle kiss, filled with sadness rather than urgency. She sighed softly as she pulled away.

"I'm really going to miss you."

I didn't answer. But I was certainly going to miss her, too. If this worked. There was still that *if*.

Hasty reminded us of his presence by rubbing his flank against our legs. Rachel reached down to pat him, then knelt to scruff his ears. "Yes, Hasty. I'm definitely going to miss you, as well!"

As she rose again, I threaded my fingers through hers. "I really hope for your sake tonight's the night."

My words may have sounded encouraging, but regret somehow leached through. She didn't need to be a mind-reader to know I was hoping against hope nothing happened. I didn't want to think about walking back to the cabin alone. She'd only been here a month, but already I knew those four walls would feel empty without her.

Giving my fingers an answering squeeze, she released my hand and sat down on the ground. We'd spent quite a bit of time discussing a plan ahead of time, and had decided she needed to replicate everything from the night of her arrival as closely as possible.

Moonlight spilled through the trees as Rachel lay down in what seemed like the right spot. I moved ten feet away into the gloomy shadow of a sheltering pine, where if that time-altering magic *were* summoned, I hopefully wouldn't be swept along with it.

As I watched, Rachel grasped the necklace in her fingers, holding it up to the sky and rotating the crystal slowly, trying to catch the moon's rays.

The gem sparkled a bit. I even thought I saw one tiny burst of light, like a flicker of spark, between her fingers. We waited, the minutes ticking by. But nothing else happened.

Propping herself up on her elbows, Rachel frowned. "Maybe we should try the glassware?"

I nodded. Dropping the pack I'd been carrying to the ground, I pulled out eight glass canning jars. Rachel had speculated those might help catch the moon's pale light, like we experienced inside the pantry. I set the jars on the ground around her as she lay back down, eyes following my movements.

"Okay. Give it another try."

I backed up.

Again, Rachel raised the crystal toward the sky, fingers slowly twisting it in the moonlight.

Still nothing.

Rachel lay still for several moments. Then abruptly she sat up, huffing her disappointment.

"What am I doing wrong? What's missing?"

I crouched beside her, forearms on my thighs. "The only thing I can see that's really different is there's no storm tonight. No lightning, like there was when this all started."

She nodded thoughtfully. "You're right. Though from what Charity told me, lightning doesn't always seem to be necessary."

She was silent for a heartbeat, then tapped a finger beside her lips. "Ah. Maybe it can be many different things – lightning, or a solstice or equinox, or who knows what other kind of planetary alignment. But apparently it isn't *just* the moon and the crystal. There needs to be some other kind of celestial energy."

"Or maybe it's just too soon."

"What do you mean?"

Moving closer, I settled an arm around her shoulder. "I have the feeling you came here for a reason. That *I* got to meet you for a reason." Gently, I rested my forehead against hers. "Maybe we just haven't figured out what that reason is, yet."

Her breath was warm against my cheek. And, slowly, slowly, I felt her arms circle my neck. Our lips met again, and this time it was infused with a hunger I hadn't felt before. Fire spiraled from my belly up through my chest, as if she'd sparked a burning ember inside me and was fanning it into a flame.

Rachel melted into me, our hands and bodies tangling. Seconds melted into what felt like eternity. And then she pulled away.

Not completely away; her hands still were laced behind my neck. But her eyes found mine, and dark though it was, I could read the reluctance there.

"Lucas, we can't do this," she breathed. "I can't – I just can't get involved with you. Not like this. I know we have to wait to figure this out better. Sooner or later, I'll try again. And yes, part of me wishes I could stay here with you. But I need to go back. I can't choose anything else. My sister needs me."

The burning in my chest suddenly turned to cold anger. Once again, I was being rejected. Once again, what I could offer wasn't good enough. Or was there someone in the future she hadn't told me about? I'd certainly kept my own secrets. Maybe Rachel had them, too.

I pushed abruptly to my feet, the heat that had engulfed me just moments ago now stone-cold.

"Yeah. I understand."

Quickly, I gathered up the canning jars and stuffed them back in the rucksack. Rachel apparently decided to risk being spotted in her outlandish garb; she didn't bother to change back into her long skirt.

Side by side we walked back to the cabin, our gazes averted, hands not touching. The silence between us seemed to ring with bitter accusation.

Or was it simply secrets.

Chapter 9

RACHEL

I stuffed the remains of our lunch back in the hamper and closed the lid.

The *Meteor*'s paddlewheel had already begun backing, her stern swinging slowly toward the dock at Rowland's. Dock-hands stood braced near the cleats, waiting to catch tossed lines as we inched closer.

Standing, I pressed my stomach against the hard metal railing, scanning the crowd lining the dock for the face I least wanted to see.

He wasn't here yet. Good.

I was nervous how it would go today. But at least Lucas was trying.

The air was still cold, but the sun warmed my cheeks while the fresh wind off the lake swept my skirts against my legs. Not bad at all for late March.

Two months left to go before I could make another try at time-hopping. I'd forced myself to come to terms with being stuck here far longer than I liked. The fifth of June still seemed terribly far away. But that was the day to try: a full moon near the summer solstice.

In the meantime, I'd resigned myself to making the best of things here. So I reminded myself that that the sun felt good; the weather blessedly mild. Near the shoreline only a few scattered patches of white remained; most of the snow had already gone off.

Hasty's wet nose nudged my fingers, then he slid his eyes toward the hamper. Subtle he was not. Chuckling, I lifted the lid of the wicker basket at my feet.

"All right, all right. I'm sure there's one more piece of ham in here with your name on it!" I dug around until I found him his treat, then insisted he sit before I tossed the bit of meat in the air. Hasty gobbled it down with a snap.

Descending the ladder from the upper deck, Lucas approached me.

"You ready?" I asked.

"Ready as I'll ever be." He smiled but his adam's apple bobbed. A sign of stress.

We bid a temporary good-bye to Hasty, entrusting him to a crew member until we returned to the ship. Threading the handle of our lunch basket over one arm, Lucas snatched up the valise I'd brought along for my change of clothes. Gallantly, he extended his elbow and we made our way toward the gangplank.

Normally I would have no trouble navigating the angled plank to the dock. But my long skirts made such obvious trip-hazards I found myself grateful once again for Lucas's steadying presence. Courtesy hadn't died yet in the Victorian era. Probably because it had life-saving properties.

We clambered aboard the train, leaving the bustling camp of Rowland's behind. Lucas seemed upbeat, and the train ride proved to be a clanking, swaying delight as the cars ferried us through rolling terrain and snatches of forest. Roughly an hour later, the engine bell clanged to announce our arrival at another logging camp - near what would later become Meyers.

But as we pulled into the siding and I took in our surroundings, my mood sank. Here, too, much of the old growth was quickly being logged off. It broke my heart to see so much of the forest gone. The hills were littered with stumps, some of them as big around as my dining table back home.

Lucas held my elbow as I stepped down from the train, his eyes scanning the crowd. Meanwhile my own stomach was churning.

"He's here." Lucas' voice beside my ear was low. He inclined his head to our left.

Indeed he was. A dozen yards away, Sullivan lounged against a wagon, an unlit cheroot dangling from his lips. Pushing himself off, he started to amble in our direction.

"You told him already that you want to renegotiate the loan?"

"I just told him I wanted to meet." Lucas set my small valise on the ground beside his feet and handed wicker picnic basket to me. His voice was chipper. "Worst he can say is no, right?"

I touched his arm. "Good luck."

But Sullivan was upon us.

"Top o' the morning, ma'am." Fingers flicked the brim of his hat while leering eyes fixed on me. "What a pleasure to see you again."

It was hardly a pleasure for me, so I didn't answer. Just shifted my gaze to Lucas.

"I understand you two have business to discuss. Shall I meet you back here in, say, an hour?"

"Sounds perfect, my dear." Lucas gave me a light peck on the cheek and bent to pick up the valise. Turning to Sullivan, he gestured toward a small wooden shack nearby with "Restaurant" scrawled in large, slanting letters over the door. "Shall we?"

I didn't have a good feeling about this meeting. But as Lucas kept repeating, nothing ventured, nothing gained. And really, what would it hurt for Sullivan to give Lucas a bit more time to repay the loan? Maybe he *would* be amenable to an extension.

Facing an hour's worth of time to kill, I began to wander the perimeter of the camp. The huge dusty flat with its giant stacks of logs was bordered by the remains of the primeval forest, shadows still pooling at the feet of proud, doomed giants. Dozens of white canvas tents dotted the edge of the camp. But activity inside the circle itself seemed somehow subdued, different from the bustling transfer camp by the lake.

The stacks of logs were smaller here, for one thing. And not as numerous. Fewer men scampered about. Not far from the restaurant half-a-dozen workers occupied a large wagon bed, bags at their feet and grim expressions on their faces.

Suddenly the picture became all too clear. The prime timber this far south wasn't exhausted, yet. But as the Comstock's voracious appetite for wood waned, timber contracts had started waning, too. Already, workmen were beginning to look for jobs elsewhere.

Stubborn as he was, Lucas clearly wasn't about to throw in the towel. But for anyone willing to read the stark writing on the wall, the message was plain to see. Only an optimist or a fool would think that timber was going to make a quick rebound. And Sullivan was neither.

Slowly I continued my circuit around the camp, allowing the sands of the hourglass to slip through. Lucas was waiting for me beside the railroad track when I returned, picnic basket at his feet and my valise still in hand. His expression was grim.

To my disappointment, Sullivan was still here, too. I spotted him lounging against a small shack a dozen feet way. Was he waiting for the same train?

Sullivan seemed to be taking a perverse interest in me, his head cocked thoughtfully to one side. What was he thinking?

Turning to face him, I stared Sullivan boldly in the eye. Rather than wince or look away, he merely turned his lips up in a small smirk.

It was Lucas who finally took my arm, drawing me farther down the tracks to add distance between us.

"I really don't like that man. There's just something about him. The way he looks at me –"

Lucas's grip on my elbow tightened. I glanced up quickly.

"I take it your conversation didn't go well?"

His eyes were looking straight ahead. "You take it right."

Thankfully, the train arrived soon, so we didn't have long to wait. I didn't see Sullivan board, but he must have secured a seat in another car. At least I didn't have to look at him during the journey.

Our ride back to Rowland's was far more subdued than the journey here. Lucas didn't elaborate on his meeting, and I thought it best to give him time to organize his thoughts before I pelted him with questions. But his eyes looked sad.

No, I thought. Not sad. *Worried.*

Sullivan had that effect on both of us. I shivered, remembering the way Sullivan had studied me before we boarded the train. Did Sullivan have designs on more than just Lucas's property?

Suddenly another, even more distressing thought seized me. Was he inspecting me like a bug under a microscope for a completely different reason? Could Sullivan have gotten an inkling I *don't belong* here?

Our plan had been to attend a dance that night being given at Rowland's before re-boarding the *Meteor* for our journey home across the lake. After his unproductive talk with Sullivan, I knew Lucas probably didn't feel much like dancing. Still, I hoped the dance would be a diversion to take his mind off his troubles and lift his spirits temporarily, at least. And things always looked brighter the next morning, right? Well, I hoped so.

Lucas wasn't talking.

Clouds had been building all late afternoon, and a strange dampness hung in the air as we stepped off the train at Rowland's about suppertime. The dance was to be at the Customs House, a sturdy wooden building occupying the end of a pier jutting over the lake.

A few tall pines still studded the nearby cove, a sight that oddly lifted my spirits. Someone had insisted on sparing those few giants, at least.

Thomas Rowland and his wife, Sophronia, had purchased this lakeside spot twenty years ago, Lucas explained, after an earlier stationhouse there had burned. Since then, a small constellation of wooden buildings had sprouted, now known collectively as Rowland's. Included were both the popular Customs House saloon where the dance would be held, and a substantial two-story inn set back from the water. Thomas Rowland wouldn't be here to greet us; he'd passed away four years ago, Lucas explained. But his wife Sophronia was still here, running the business.

And sure enough, our hostess was there to greet us when we stepped inside the inn. After a brief whisper from Lucas in her ear, she whisked me off upstairs so I could change into the fancier dress and shoes I'd brought with me in the valise. Thank heavens yet again for Charity and her thoughtful gifts of clothing!

Before I knew it, Lucas was escorting me up the wooden stairs to the top floor of the Customs House. A five-man string band had struck up a bouncy tune inside the cavernous dance hall, and the party was already in full swing.

Lucas's face remained solemn. But he took my hand, leading me out onto the dance floor. I hoped he could leave his troubles behind for the time being.

I wasn't much for ballroom dancing, but Lucas proved a fine dancer and it was easy enough to follow the simple steps. Before long, I felt myself finally starting to relax in his arms. It had been a stressful day, and I still worried about Lucas's financial future. But for the moment at least, we both were smiling.

We made a good pair on the dance floor. He pulled me closer as the room grew crowded, his hand tightening on my back. I didn't mind a bit. I found my thoughts drifting back to the kiss we'd shared in the moonlight a few weeks ago, that night when I'd tried unsuccessfully to return home. So much had changed between us.

In just a few more weeks more I'd be attempting to reverse the time-magic again. It seemed like terrible timing, with Lucas's finances in such dire straits. Leaving him to face that alone felt wrong. I kept hoping he'd be alright when I was gone.

It was a worry that begged the real question, of course: whether I should leave at all. Charity, after all, had made the decision to stay right here in the Victorian era. And to be honest, I'd toyed with that same notion myself. But every time I started down that mental road, Serena popped to mind.

My sister needed me. She might even need me now more than ever. As adept as Serena was at finding trouble, who knew what messes she might have conjured up while I was gone?! *Of course* I needed to go back. I just needed to figure out precisely how.

Breathless after an hour of dancing, I allowed Lucas to lead me toward the refreshment table. Ahead of us in line was a tall, stiff-postured man, balding on top with a neatly-trimmed ring of grey hair below. A stately woman in her late 40s stood beside him. The pair turned with smiles as we approached.

"Russell! I just heard the happy matrimonial news. You must introduce us to your lovely wife."

Lucas settled a palm on the curve of my back, a subtly possessive gesture that somehow made me relax. "Sweetheart,

I'd like to introduce Mr. and Mrs. D.L. Bliss." He turned to smile at the tall man again. "And you're exactly right, Bliss. This is my new – wife, Rachel."

A round of polite bows and curtseys followed.

Had Lucas stumbled slightly over the word 'wife'? If so, I was too dumbstruck to pay much heed. This man with the natty bowtie and prominent nose – this was *the* D.L. Bliss, the timber giant? The man who in years to come would help turn Lake Tahoe into a recreational mecca? And this self-assured woman was Bliss's wife, Elizabeth. I could hardly believe I was rubbing shoulders with such famous people!

Bliss was clapping Lucas heartily on the shoulder. "Too bad Old Monk can't be here with us tonight for the festivities, eh?"

"Yes. A shame to lose a good man like that. But I suppose he's in a better place."

"True enough," Bliss chuckled. "Though from what I hear, he was already so well-pickled no embalming was needed."

I vaguely recalled that Hank Monk had died in 1883. So I'd missed meeting that famous figure, too, by only four years. Pneumonia had taken the iconic stage driver, I'd read. Pneumonia complicated by heavy drinking, apparently.

The string band took a break just then to join our line for a little imbibing of their own. That, at least, made for easier conversation. And before long the discussion with Bliss turned, of course, to the current downturn in lumber.

"It'll turn around," Lucas insisted gamely. "Another big strike at the mines and timber will be booming again."

Bliss just shook his head. "You must remember, my boy, that lumber is a finite commodity. But pleasure cruises and opportunities for recreation? Ah, both supply and demand are infinite for *those* here at Tahoe!"

Lucas's face fell. It hadn't been what he'd wanted to hear. Especially after his disappointing meeting earlier today with Sullivan.

After a few more dances, he edged us toward the door. "I hear thunder in the distance. Probably best we be going."

I was fine with leaving. It had been a long day. And Lucas probably needed time to figure out his next step after his unproductive meeting with Sullivan. We said our good-byes and soon made our way to the dock.

Hasty greeted us with enthusiastic circles as we stepped back aboard the *Meteor*.

"Come on, boy." Lucas hefted the dog under one arm, then waved me ahead up the narrow metal stairs to the upper deck.

Setting Hasty back on his feet at the top, Lucas loosened his tie and sank down on a bench, long legs extended in front of him. Hasty curled at his feet, head on his paws.

Glad to have a chance to rest, I took a seat beside Lucas on the bench. His arm threaded around my shoulder, pulling me gently against his side. For the longest time we just sat there in companionable silence, staring out at the stars playing hide-and-seek in the clouds over the lake.

"He was right, you know." I touched my fingers gently to Lucas's cheek, coaxing him to turn his head to look at me.

"Who's right?"

"Bliss. He was right about Tahoe's future being tourism and recreation."

Lucas pushed my hand away and leaned forward. "All I know is logging. What do you want me to do. Sell out for whatever I can get and just give up?"

"Why does it have to be all or nothing? Maybe you could sell off just a small piece of your land. Then maybe you could turn this boat into a pleasure craft to take visitors around the lake? Others are doing it. You said so yourself."

He stood, jamming his hands in his pockets. "So you believe that that's the future. Like Bliss. Well, maybe you're right. But maybe the future of Tahoe you *think* you know won't come to pass. Maybe the simple fact that you're here, right now—that you somehow came back in time—maybe that's changed everything. Maybe right now the future you think you know doesn't even exist."

I shuddered. Could he be right? What if my voyage through time accidentally altered not only the future I hoped to return to, but my sister's future, too? Was Serena *even still alive?*

But Lucas wasn't finished. His fingers formed fists at his side. "Timber land - that's all I have. And much as you say it's not the future, right now it's what I have. I've staked everything on it. It's too late for me to change course."

I rose from the bench, my face warming despite the chill wind blowing across the lake.

"Too late to change course now? When you're headed straight for a cliff and still have time to put on the brakes? Lucas, be reasonable!"

I threw a hand in the air in disgust. "You told me yourself that Sullivan will probably wind up with everything you own in a few short months. Much as you want things to be different, demand for lumber *hasn't* picked up. You heard Bliss this evening. Why continue to just cross your fingers and hang onto a dream that isn't working? Why not at least try something different?"

Our voices had risen, attracting curious stares. From the corner of my eye I saw a pair of crewmen studying us.

But I'd inadvertently ripped open an old wound, and Lucas wasn't about to let it go.

"Trust me, my brother has told me over and over my whole adult life what a fool I've been." Bitterness oozed from his voice. "First, for trying my hand at silver mining. Then for investing in Tahoe timber. 'A huge mistake,' he kept saying. 'Cattle. That's what you should be doing, just like me.' And you know what? My brother was probably right. He's got a wife, a family, and a great spread of land. And all I've got is hope." He paused. "I've worked too hard to get here, Rachel. I can't throw in the towel. There's still a few months left. . ."

Ah. I finally understood. Lucas had already branded himself a failure. He was bracing himself for an impact he didn't know how to avoid. Like a captain preparing to go down with his ship. As if his honor was the last piece he could hope to salvage.

"I never said you should throw in the towel completely. For once, Lucas, try to see beyond your own stubbornness. All I'm saying is, times change. Goals need to change accordingly. I'm not saying you ought to give up. But maybe you could sell just a small piece of land. Invest in something different. Think recreation instead of logging."

A sudden thunderclap interrupted us. The clouds that had been building all day finally opened up, rain sheeting down by the bucketful. Thankfully we were protected from the worst of the deluge by the wooden canopy over the ship's upper deck. But the wind off the lake began whipping across the deck, depositing a fine layer of moisture on our clothes and hair.

Off to my left a jagged bolt of lightning split the heavens above the water, followed almost immediately by another loud *cr-raaack!*

Hasty was on his feet beside us, legs apart, ears back.

"Come on. We best be getting out of the weather." One hand on my back, Lucas herded us back toward the stairs, then stooped to pick up Hasty. "Quick, now."

Another crack of thunder echoed just as my feet reached the metal surface of the lower deck. My hand still clutched the metal railing of the staircase, and a strange buzzing spun through my fingers. Tucked against my chest, the crystal pendant seemed to be buzzing slightly, too. Releasing the rail I turned – to encounter the strangest sight I'd ever seen.

Lightning continued to flash intermittently through the clouds over the water. But now the ship itself was wrapped in a luminous green glow. From the deck to the railing to the bodies of the crewmen at their stations, everything sported an eerie halo of bluish-green light. Even the lake wore a sheen or mist of luminous particles on its surface.

Hasty growled softly at Lucas's feet. A great, glowing ball of light enveloped the dog, too. Instinctively I reached out a hand to touch it, only to pull it sharply back with a cry – my fingers felt like I'd touched a hot electrical wire.

Lucas's eyes were wide with wonder. "St. Elmo's fire! I've never seen it on the lake before!"

I'd heard of St. Elmo's fire. A peculiar energy associated with electrical storms, it was a not uncommon phenomenon reported by ocean-going sailors. Like Lucas, I'd never heard of it occurring on a lake before, though.

Before long, the odd glow began to fade. Minutes later, it was gone. But the strong wind was still whipping the surface of the lake into whitecaps, and the heavy rain hadn't abated.

Seemingly immune to the white-topped waves, the *Meteor* forged her way gallantly through the chop toward the dock. And before I knew it, Lucas's fingers were wrapping mine as he guided me down the gangplank at Glenbrook.

A small shock went through me at his gentle touch, a sensation that had nothing to do with St. Elmo's fire. Did he feel it, too? He continued to hold my hand a few seconds after we'd reached the wooden dock, then silently released me.

Hasty stepped gingerly down the gangplank behind us, then leaped the last drop to the dock. He shook himself heartily, flecks of dampness from his fur spraying everywhere. I took that to mean he was happy to be home.

Lucas lifted his eyes to the clouds still pelting us with rain, then settled an arm around my shoulder. "Come on. We're going to have to run for it." Laughing, we dashed for the cabin, the gusting wind helping drive us forward. Within minutes, all three of us were soaked.

Lucas and I were still grinning ear-to-ear when we reached the cabin, puddles forming on the floor at our feet as we finally closed the door behind us. Hasty gave another heroic shake, spreading the unmistakable odor of wet doggie fur.

"That was quite an amazing display by Mother Nature!" Lucas shook his head, seating himself on the floor to tug off his wet boots. "And she just might have given us the key we've been waiting for."

I wasn't following.

His smile widened. "There was lightning on the night we both made our unexpected leap in time, if you'll remember."

I stared down at him, thoughts shuffling through my brain like a mismatched deck of cards as I tried to make sense of what he'd just said.

All of a sudden it fell into place. "So, you think Mother Nature – lightning – is my ticket home?"

Grabbing my hands, he pulled me gently down until I was sitting across his lap.

"I'm all wet!"

"So am I."

And before I knew it, his mouth was on mine again. A warm, sweet kiss, full of happiness. And perhaps so much more.

Placing both hands gently on his cheeks, I finally pulled away. My heart thumped loudly in my ears, though whether it was from that kiss or the exciting insight he'd just shared, I really couldn't say. Maybe both.

"So, lightning's the power I need to get me back home?"

His eyes twinkled. "I'm thinking so. The problem is, of course, that Mother Nature's fireworks tend be all over the sky on nights like this. So hoping for lightning to strike extremely close, like it did with us that night – well, it's a terrible long-shot. You could be waiting for the right conditions for a really, really long time."

"But if a lightning storm like that happened at the full moon –" My voice was rising with excitement.

"Exactly. If a lightning storm coincided with the full moon, perhaps the *Meteor*'s metal deck would draw that awesome power to itself."

"Like it did tonight!" I grabbed his hands, exuberant.

"Just like it did tonight." He squeezed my fingers back, his grin mirroring mine.

A silence descended, as we both contemplated what that meant.

I had it, now. The way to make the reverse leap to my own time. A way to return to everything I'd left behind.

Then, slowly, inexorably, as if a magnet was pulling us together, I was in Lucas' arms again.

I couldn't help myself. Yes, I'd told him I didn't want this. I was lying.

Right now, kissing Lucas felt right. As right and natural as day follows night, and night follows day. As much a part of the rhythm of my life as breathing.

His lips were soft at first, then insistent. My arms wound their way around his neck as they moved if their own accord. My fingers traced his jaw and tangled in his hair. I couldn't get enough of the textures of him.

And then, just when I felt like I never, *ever* wanted to stop kissing Lucas Russell, I pulled away. He looked down, hurt dawning on his face. Our fingers trailed away from each other.

I sighed, and touched a gentle finger to those wonderful lips I'd just been kissing. An apology. A promise I would never forget tonight. I wanted this. So much, I wanted – well, everything with him. I wanted to stay a part of Lucas Russell's life. I wanted more.

But whatever this was between us, there was, quite literally, no future in it. My life, my future, was elsewhere. In an all-too-distant century.

"I'm sorry." I rose to standing, brushing my hands across the damp folds of my dress.

Sadly, deliberately, he stood as well. The distance between us now had nothing to do with feet or inches.

Turning to the woodstove, Lucas began to quietly stoke up the fire.

He needed time, I told myself. Eventually he'd see it was all for the best.

A tear broke loose and tumbled down my cheek. I brushed it angrily away.

Sagging to the edge of the bed, I shucked off my wet shoes and peeled down my soaked stockings. Using a towel from the cupboard, I managed to wring some of the excess moisture from my hair.

What he'd suggested about time travel made sense. Using the *Meteor* to draw energy from an electrical storm could be exactly the accelerator I needed to leap back through time. Back to my own century. Back to my sister.

It all depended on a happy confluence of celestial events, of course – a full moon, a storm, perhaps a solstice. But it had all obviously happened before. This could really work!

So why did my stomach suddenly feel as if I'd swallowed a bar of lead?

Chapter 10

LUCAS

Four more days. Four more days. That phrase kept echoing through my head as my feet turned toward home, Hasty trotting contentedly at my heels. One of us, at least, was happy.

Four.

More.

Days.

No storm had put in an appearance during the full moons of April and May. And without a solstice or a storm to help, we hadn't even bothered to try.

But the full moon of June fifth was nearly upon us. Rachel had been getting increasingly excited, bustling about the cabin with a smile on her face, while I was getting increasingly – well, *what?* Nervous? Scared? *'Grumpy'* probably summed it up best.

And torn. That was another word that fit. I felt split in half, with strong feelings on both sides. On the one hand, I wanted to do everything I could to help Rachel get home again. Back to her sister. Back to the life she used to know.

But at the same time, I kept thinking about what my own life would look like if she succeeded.

When she succeeded, I corrected myself. Because sooner or later, all the pieces *would* fall into place. If not at this full moon, then another. Eventually, the same magic confluence that swept her here would sweep her away from me again.

Halting my steps at the cast-iron scraper by the cabin door, I knocked the worst of the caked-on dirt from my boots before entering. Hasty trailed me inside, making a bee-line for his water bowl. It had been warm at the lake today.

I sniffed, then sniffed again. A heavenly scent greeted me; whatever Rachel was making for dinner smelled amazing.

Her touch was everywhere, I realized, my eyes scanning the cabin. She'd reorganized my kitchen; a wide array of spices and cooking supplies now lined the once-meager shelves. Pine needle baskets dotted the room, holding everything from spools of thread to pencils to soap. She'd worked out an arrangement with a woman in the village, so we had all the fresh milk and eggs we could eat in trade for Rachel's teas and salves. She'd even cajoled me into trying wild foods like nettles and pine needle tea. And her bread! Every meal brought some fresh delight.

I'd tried to convince myself that having the cabin to myself again would be a relief. My head would be clearer, there'd be less distraction, more time to focus on what my next steps should be. All a complete lie, of course. I'd grown used to Rachel's company. . . her laugh. . . her unfailing encouragement. Coming home to an empty cabin was going to feel. . . well, *empty.*

Then again, it wouldn't be mine for long. My loan was coming due the end of this month. Sullivan had been finding excuses to show up at the dock once or twice a week. While he hadn't said a word, he'd worn an ear-to-ear grin every time I bumped into him. The thought that I'd soon be losing my cabin to him on top of everything else made my stomach churn.

Rolling up my sleeves, I turned to the wash basin and dipped my hands and forearms in the cool water, splashing away the dust and dirt of the day. From her post at the woodstove, Rachel turned a wan smile my way.

"Everything go okay today?" she asked, lifting a wooden ladle from the pot.

"Fine." I pasted on a happy face and took my usual seat at the table. Plates had already been set out, awaiting tonight's masterpiece. No use burdening her with my worries.

Soon, I'd have to move on, go elsewhere – to the coast, perhaps. Try to find a job. Start over. If I'd only listened to my brother in the first place, perhaps things might have been different. Not that cattle-raising had ever been my cup of tea. And if I hadn't been here, I never would have met Rachel.

Four more days. With luck, Rachel would be home with her sister again before my own financial disaster hit. As long as she was happy. That's really all that mattered.

Something about Rachel drew my eyes to her face again. She seemed off tonight. Tired, her eyes drooping. Sure, she'd been cooking at a hot stove. But her cheeks seemed surprisingly flushed.

"You feeling okay?"

She didn't answer. Her body swayed.

I was on my feet again in seconds and across the room, a steadying hand on her shoulder. Gently, I pressed the back of one hand to her forehead, then her cheek.

"Rachel! You're burning up."

RACHEL

It wasn't like me to fall into bed before dinner. But the fever really had taken the starch out of me.

Lucas had tucked me in and insisted I stay under the blankets even though the cabin was plenty warm. And he hadn't moved from the ladderback chair at my bedside. For the umpteenth time in the last hour he reached over to feel my forehead, then urged me to drink more water.

I forced myself to take a few sips just to make him happy, though I wasn't really thirsty. And I certainly wasn't hungry.

Concern was etched in his eyes. And that look touched something deep inside me.

I'd already fallen for Lucas Russell. Hard. An awareness I'd been battling for months. He was a good man, a kind man. And tonight, his gentleness only made me fall harder, if that was possible.

That look of worry creased his face. Perhaps I should be worried, too. I felt limp as a dishrag. But fever can do that to you. The only worrying part was that it didn't seem to be coming down.

Lacing my fingers through his atop the blanket, I finally asked what was worrying me most of all.

"Your loan's almost due, and I know you've been fretting. Have you decided what you are going to do?"

He sighed, shifting in his chair. "Not much choice, really. Leave Tahoe and find work where I can, I guess. Start over."

"But where?"

His eyes shifted away. "The Central Valley, maybe." One hand skated through the hair at the nape of his neck in frustration. "Honestly, I don't know, yet. But I'll figure it out."

"Have you thought at all about what Bliss was saying? About other possibilities right here at Tahoe. Fishing, boating, recreation?"

Lucas bent forward and brushed a strand of hair from my forehead. The action was sweet, almost tender. But his gaze had shuttered.

His fingers squeezed mine. "Don't you worry about me. Just concentrate on getting well."

He craned his head toward the shelves on the far wall, then his eyes dropped to mine again. "You doctored up my hand just fine. Isn't there something over there that might help you?"

I squelched the ridiculous urge to pump a fist in the air, but did allow myself a grin. He'd just conceded I *did* know something about medicine and plants! But he was genuinely worried. Not a time to be chuckling over my small victory.

At my direction, Lucas pulled down a bag of willow bark and brewed a steaming cup of tea for me. It helped ease the body ache, though not for long. As night came I grew increasingly feverish. Mint tea, willow tea, feverfew—nothing seemed to bring the fever down. I slept and woke; slept and woke. Each time, Lucas was there by my bedside when I opened my eyes.

Sometime late that night I awakened to see the nearly-full moon cresting the treetops outside the window. Lucas was still there in the chair, a quilt over his legs. Wide awake. A crazy-worried expression on his face.

Groggily, I reached for his hand. In an instant he was there, gripping my fingers while he tugged the covers up at my neck with the other.

"I'm worried about you."

He'd kept a small lamp burning on the bedside table, shedding a thin circle of light around us - and what I saw when I looked in his eyes surprised me. He was worried because he cared.

I let my eyes drift toward the window again, processing this new revelation. Was it true? Had Lucas grown to care for me the way I cared about him? A strange flutter ran through my belly.

As I watched, the moon continued slowly rising, rising, casting shadows across the room. Random clouds scudded across its surface, though heaven only knew if a storm would follow. The full moon I was waiting for was only a few days away, now - close to the summer solstice.

Would I be well enough to *try* a time-leap then? And what would I find if I managed to get home again? What disaster could Serena have manufactured in the three long months I'd been gone?

So many *ifs*: *If* the full moon and a storm overlapped. *If* Lucas was right about the metal *Meteor* channeling the lightning's energy. And now *if* I managed to recover in time to make the attempt.

I bit the inside of my cheek. I had to get well. I *had* to try to get home.

Lucas patted my hand and rose to tend the fire. I watched his muscles flex beneath his shirt as he bent to add a small log to the flames, though it was already plenty warm in the cabin.

My eyelids kept trying to drift closed but I fought the feeling, determined to keep swimming back to consciousness. Was it the tea making me so sleepy, or the fever?

I didn't know. Didn't care.

I struggled to make sense of all the thoughts in my head. Snippets of memories; bits and pieces of the good times I'd had since I got here. The shivaree. Sailing across the sparkling waves of the lake aboard the *Meteor*. Teasing Lucas about his grumpy disposition. Whipping up hearty stews and breads in the cabin's small kitchen – the smile on Lucas's face every evening.

Hasty interrupted my thoughts by padding over and sticking his snout in my dangling hand. Smiling, I scratched his ears. If this really worked – if I *did* get home – I'd miss Hasty. I'd miss this cabin. My burgeoning friendship with Charity, and all the neighbors I'd met here. I'd bring with me enough adventurous memories to last a lifetime, of course. But memories wouldn't be the same.

Most of all, I'd miss Lucas. It was difficult to imagine a day going by without him. Somehow, he'd worked his way under my skin and straight into my heart. And just like he worried about me, I worried about him, as well. What would become of him after I left? Where would he go? Would he go over the mountains to the Central Valley, as he'd suggested, or perhaps to the coast?

I wouldn't be here to help in the difficult months and years to come. To offer support and encouragement. To remind him he was every bit as good as his brother. I was confident Lucas could be a success at whatever he put his mind to. Lucas didn't seem to share that belief, and that made me incredibly sad.

We'd kissed twice – an experience I'd have given anything to repeat. But neither of us had ever used the word 'love.'

That was the word that kept springing to mind, though, whenever I thought of Lucas. I'd fought to tamp down the feeling, knowing I had to leave. My sister needed me. I had to go back. Had to at least *try.*

But yes, I thought, as my eyes drifted closed again. *Love.* I'm in love with Lucas Russell.

And our time together was coming to an end.

Maybe it was the willow bark tea. Maybe it was my own sheer determination, prompted by that glimpse of the full moon through the window. Or maybe the fever simply ran its course.

Whatever the healing magic, by next morning I was able to sit up in bed. And by late afternoon, I was up and walking somewhat shakily around the cabin.

The following day, Lucas felt confident enough in my recovery to leave me alone for a few hours while he went to town for a few supplies. It was a warm June morning, and I felt ready to stretch my legs. I wouldn't walk far; just down the road and back.

Hasty gave a short bark as I opened the front door, demanding to come along. With a laugh, I shooed him through the doorway ahead of me.

The pale echo of last night's moon still hung in the sky as we started off. Its nearly-full shape reminding me yet again that the window for time-travel was opening. Perhaps even tonight, if a storm happened to show up.

A quick glance at the sky told me – yes! Clouds were forming over the lake. Tonight or tomorrow – it might just work!

I should be ecstatic, right? Yet as I turned to head back to the cabin again I found my steps slowing. I was leaving all this, once and for all. I had my sister to finish raising. Pieces of a life to pick back up.

And what would I find when I did get back home? I twisted my lower lip in my teeth. No way to really know until I got back.

Something about the cabin felt wrong as I got closer. I was certain I'd shut the door firmly when Hasty and I left. Yet now the cabin door stood ajar.

"Hello? Anyone here?" I called. I pushed the door open and stepped cautiously inside, Hasty at my heels.

My eyes took a minute to adjust to the gloom. But when they did, I my eyebrows nearly hit the ceiling.

A well-dressed woman was seated in Lucas's chair at the kitchen table, hands clasped casually over the folds of her striped silk gown. A very pretty, *young* woman, flaxen curls arranged just so. A hat with a large feather plume sat casually on the table beside her.

She'd made herself to home.

Hasty sniffed the hem of the woman's skirt, then padded off to curl up in his usual spot on a blanket. She wasn't a stranger, apparently.

The blonde turned a steely gaze on me, head bobbing as she slowly looked me up and down. "Who are you?!"

Who was I? She acted as if she had every right to be here. And Hasty certainly recognized her. One of Lucas's relatives, perhaps?

I thought fast. Best keep up the fiction we'd created.

"I'm Lucas Russell's wife." It took an effort, but I managed to school my features. "And you are–?"

"His *wife?!*" It was a shrill bark. The woman jumped to her feet. Face flushed, she bent toward me, hands on her hips. "There must be some mistake. For your information, I'm Lucas Russell's fiancée!"

Lucas strode through the door at that precise moment, a bag of groceries in his arms. His eyes darkened as he took in the woman standing nearly nose-to-nose with me.

"Amanda! What are you doing here?"

So. Her name was Amanda. And he *did* know her.

The woman inched back, then pointed a long, slim finger at me. "What is *she* doing here?" It was another screech.

Lucas set his bag of groceries on the table and the woman turned toward him. "She claims she's your *wife*. Lucas, this can't be! How *could* you?!"

Her lower lip trembled. I fully expected we'd be treated to a torrent of tears any second.

"You left, Amanda –"

The woman cut him off, a snarl contorting those pretty features. "I'll sue you for breach of promise, Lucas Russell! You led me on!" Her right hand flashed out, pushing him in the chest, hard. A piece of me felt inappropriately gratified to see Lucas didn't budge an inch.

"I have a witness, as you well know! Sylvester was there. He'll testify that you promised to marry me."

Sylvester Sullivan had witnessed Lucas' marriage proposal to this woman?

The mention of a lawsuit and witnesses was no idle threat, I knew. Breach-of-promise suits were a serious matter in the Victorian age. With no money for Lucas to defend himself and a witness in her corner, this woman would hold the legal upper hand. And she knew it.

"That was a long time ago, Amanda. You're the one who took off nearly a year ago without so much as the courtesy of a note. I figured you'd left with another man!"

The blonde tossed her head. "You can't prove that. And I still have my witness."

Ah. So she wasn't denying that she'd left with someone else.

A horrified expression had settled over Lucas's features. He threw a quick glance at me, his eyes pleading. For patience, for understanding.

I managed to keep a calm façade. But inside, a volcano was erupting.

Lucas never told me that he'd been engaged. And according to this woman, he was *still* engaged.

He'd not only deceived me, he'd deliberately pulled the wool over his neighbors' eyes as well with his lie that we were married.

I obviously didn't know the man who stood before me as well as I had thought. If he hadn't bothered to tell me about a fiancée, what *else* hadn't he told me?

I could have kicked myself for being so horribly disappointed. Disappointed in him. Disappointed in myself for trusting him. I'd let my guard down so quickly. Trusted him. Begun to care about him.

Meanwhile, Amanda - pretty, blonde, petite Amanda - was the one he really cared about. Cared enough to have asked her to marry him, with Sullivan as a witness.

I wasn't about to stand in their way. And I wouldn't help Lucas perpetuate our "marriage" lie any longer.

Suddenly I felt frantic to escape the confining walls of the cabin. To get away. Back to the world I knew. To my own time. To normalcy. Desperate to put this whole ugly episode behind me. And hopefully, over time, eventually forget about the charming, dashing, deceitful Lucas Russell and all the time I'd spent with him.

Chapter 11

RACHEL

As it turned out, I wasn't the only one anxious to leave the cabin. The door slammed behind her as Amanda stormed out.

Lucas, I noticed, had made no effort to stop her.

He turned to face me, hands spread wide. He knew I was seething.

"Rachel, listen to me. Amanda left town suddenly over nine months ago. There was no fight, no argument, no notice. She just up and left, not even leaving me a note. I thought she'd dumped me. Honest."

I wasn't buying it. They'd been *engaged,* for heaven's sakes!

"And you just let her go, just like that? Even if she *did* leave, you should've gone after her. Tried to make it work." I gulped before throwing in the clincher. "*She* obviously still wants to make it work!"

"You don't understand." Lucas threw one hand in the air. "I couldn't simply take off. I had a business to run, men to oversee. She knew that. What was I supposed to think? She could at least have bothered to send a note!"

A note. Something clicked in the back of my brain.

That packet of letters on his bedside table. The ones with the pretty ribbon tied around them. Were those love letters from Amanda? Letters that Lucas had *kept*?

He couldn't tell me his heart wasn't still tied up with Amanda.

It explained so much. His cool reserve, the distance he always kept from me.

Those letters said it all. Secretly, he must have hoped for exactly this moment. That she'd return. That she'd still want him.

Well, he'd gotten his wish.

I felt like kicking myself all over again. How could I ever have fallen for this deceitful, dishonest man?!

"You had a business to run? That's a BS excuse and you know it."

It may not have been a Victorian expression, but Lucas obviously got my drift. Lips pressed together, he had the good grace to look sheepish.

"Look. To be completely honest, part of me was actually *relieved* when Amanda disappeared."

I stomped my foot. "But she's come back for you now, Lucas. She obviously still wants you. I won't stand in the way of that – especially because this 'marriage' you concocted is a complete fiction. She's your fiancée. You owe her the truth. That we're *not* really married. And you owe it to her to at least try to make it work."

With a huff, he turned away. "I suspect the only reason Amanda is back is because she couldn't make it work with whoever she ran off with. No, my relationship with her is over – and *she*'s the one who ended it, long before I ever met you."

Grabbing a sweater from the hook by the door, I threw it around my shoulders and tugged the door open. "I'm going for a walk."

Lucas reached out, fingers on my upper arm. "Stay. Please. We need to talk."

I shook his hand off. "No, we've talked enough. You and your *fiancée* are the ones who need to talk!"

The front door gave a final, satisfying slam behind me.

Was it possible to get so angry your heart shattered?

No, I told myself. My heart *was* shattered, and I *was* angry. But those were two separate things.

How could Lucas have hidden his relationship with Amanda from me? His *engagement* to someone else? And it wasn't only me that he'd deceived. How could he have blithely promoted the lie about us being married to his neighbors?

I would have sworn Lucas didn't have a deceitful bone in his body. Well, *before today* I would have. Now I was just so mad I could spit nails. And so hurt.

Despite everything, I couldn't stop remembering the look on his face as I'd slammed the door to the cabin. He'd looked as if he'd lost his best friend. Maybe he did. Amanda sure as shootin' hadn't returned to prop him up. No, in the short time I'd been in her presence, even I could tell the reason she came back had everything to do with what Amanda needed and very little to do with Lucas' needs.

Still, they were engaged. Or at least they had been, and neither of them had called it off. That meant they still needed to figure things out, just the two of them, without my help or interference.

Trouble was, I wasn't simply mad. Mad's something you can get over.

No, the *real* problem was that I was still head-over-heels in love with Lucas. And that was something I wasn't sure I'd ever get over.

Would he be happy with Amanda? And what would happen to him in just another few weeks, when Sullivan's loan came due? With any luck, I wouldn't still be here to find out. Still, I worried how he would fare. And that made me mad all over again. Why should I care?

Well, there was a simple enough answer for that. My stupid heart couldn't help it.

My feet had carried me to the far edge of town, where a finger of heavy woods still bordered the road. Off to my left a trail cut deeper into the forest. Without thinking, I turned onto it.

Lucas probably wasn't following me. But I wanted to make sure I'd be left alone with my thoughts.

Looking up, white clouds were mushrooming, billowing up taller and stronger than this morning, with a band of dark grey across their undersides that portended rain. A storm was blowing in. A lucky sign for getting home again soon. Tonight wasn't perfect; the moon wouldn't be completely full for another day or so. But with any luck the clouds and their moisture would hang around another day or two. If the stars and storms and signs all continued to align, I'd finally be able to get home to Serena. To 2023. And *stay* there.

Because I was thoroughly, completely done with Lucas, I told myself. Even if my stupid heart might not be.

By now my long strides had carried me deep into the woods. The canopy of branches overhead blocked out much of the sky. Off to both sides the underbrush lay deep in shadow. The gloomy setting seemed a fitting backdrop for my unhappy thoughts. But a little unnerving, too.

I thought I heard a branch snap behind me. I swiveled quickly, but saw nothing. The woods seemed as still and lonely as ever. Maybe I'd imagined it. Still, my breathing picked up. What if I ran into a bear when I was alone here out all alone?

It was nothing, I reassured myself. Bears would be as afraid of me as I was of them. And with their phenomenal sense of smell, they'd steer clear of humans.

I continued following the wooded trail, and my heart rhythm eventually settling back to normal. But as I rounded a bend in the trail a few minutes later, another snap sounded behind me. Much closer, this time. A noise I definitely wasn't imagining.

I was turning my head to look for the source when a large hand clamped solidly across my mouth.

"Don't make a noise or try to cry out," a harsh voice rasped at my ear. "You're coming with me."

Something hard pressed into my ribs. A gun, I presumed.

The face near my own swam into focus and suddenly I realized why that voice had sounded so familiar. Sylvester Sullivan wore an oily grin.

"You've been following me!"

He nodded, that cold smile stretching wider. "Watching and waiting, my dear. Watching and waiting."

Dark eyes narrowing, he pushed his face closer to mine. The pressure in my ribs increased as he leaned forward.

"And you're going to tell me your secret - exactly how you've been able to leap through time."

But Sullivan wasn't expecting an answer immediately. Pulling a length of rope from his pocket he bound my hands behind me, then produced a strip of cloth and tied it hastily across my eyes for a blindfold. Shoving that hard metal object against my ribs again, he forced me to walk in front of him, keeping one hand on my shoulder to guide me. He didn't say where we were going, but I could guess: somewhere deeper into the woods. Where he could interrogate me about time-travel at his leisure.

I stumbled twice, tripping over some unseen object on the trail and nearly falling flat on my face. Each time he roughly jerked me back on my feet.

Hours later, or at least that's how it felt, he told me to "step up," and I felt a smooth wooden surface beneath my boots. I heard the creak of a door opening, and he pushed me inside what I guessed must be a cabin. I fell hard, landing on my side, bound hands scraping against the rough floorboards. I'd long since lost my sweater, but my long skirt and petticoats provided a tiny bit of padding. Still, my hip ached. I'd probably be sporting a lovely black-and-blue mark tomorrow. If I lived that long.

"Why are you doing this, Sullivan? You're a banker, a rich man!"

"And I'll be a far richer man once I get the time-travel secret. Which stocks will go up soon? I'll own them. What railroads are going to merge? I'll be a member of that happy consortium."

I tried for offended innocence. "And what makes you think I know how to leap through time? That's crazy! It's impossible!"

His voice was a throaty chuckle at my ear. "Don't bother trying to deny it. I happened to be there at the inn that stormy night when you arrived. You and that blasted Captain Russell of yours. Just happened to be relieving myself in the bushes. The back yard was empty, and then there was a bold flash of lightning and suddenly there you both were. I saw the two of you, all chummy, there on the ground. Watched you look around, all confused-like. You didn't see me, but I could see you."

He laughed again, an ugly sound. Hot, fetid breath brushed my cheek. "I heard you ask Russell what year it was. At first I didn't believe my own ears. But then I got a good look at the odd clothes you were wearing. And since then, I've watched you carefully. Listened to the way you talk. Those odd expressions that come out of your mouth from time to time. You and that woman from Carson Valley, Charity –"

I gulped. "Charity's got nothing to do with it!"

"You both have that strangeness about you. It was hard for me to figure, at first. But over time I realized it was true. Both of you, you're *different*. And the more I thought about the way you suddenly just *appeared* and those strange clothes . . . well. I started to suspect."

I tried to roll away from him, but a hand gripped my shoulder. That stinking breath was on my face again. "And then

I overheard you two talking that day on the pier, and that confirmed it. '*When are you from?*' she asked you. Remember that?"

Oh, I remembered. But I hated the fact he was drawing Charity into this, too. What would he do to her?

"As soon as I heard that, I realized. She's a time-traveler too. Just like you."

He must have sat back on his haunches. I heard the floorboards creak. Blessedly, that awful voice came from slightly further away, no longer right by my ear. "I tried going after her a time or two, but never managed to get her alone. You, however - you were easy." That awful chuckle again. "I just had to wait for the right moment. And that moment is now."

"Okay." I decided to go with the truth. Or at least part of it. My necklace bobbed against my chest as I attempted to roll myself to a sitting position. But I'd tell him as little as I could.

"You're right. I'm from the future. But I never asked to come here, and I'm not at all sure how it happened, so I can't tell you much. And even if you manage to make a similar leap, you'd be going to a time where it'll be obvious you don't belong. It could be dangerous, or the reverse trip might not work for you at all. And if you did manage to return, you could inadvertently change the very future you're expecting to help you."

A hand gripped my chin, wrenching my head to the side while a second hand whipped off my blindfold.

Blinking, I glanced around. I was in a small cabin, alright. More of a shack, really, with open studs and barely enough headroom for a grown man to stand. No furniture except a small, rickety-looking wooden chair. One small window pierced the back wall, its sill chest-high. Outside, daylight was fading.

"I'm willing to take that chance. When opportunity knocks, it's only fools who don't listen."

Only fools don't listen. I'd been a fool, alright. How had I not seen the danger in this man? I'd never liked him, certainly. But I hadn't realized how deep the evil ran.

"You're assuming I know how the time-travel works, and I don't. As far as I can tell, it seems to have something to do with a full moon plus lightning. But some other element seems to be involved as well. I already tried once at the full moon. It didn't work."

I deliberately left out any mention of the crystal necklace or the solstice – both of which were at hand, if he only knew it.

"Don't play coy with me, girlie. I think you know far more than you're lettin' on." He huffed, hands on his hips. "I'll give you time to think it over. But you'll get nothing to eat or drink until you come up with a better answer, so you better think fast. I'll be back in the mornin' to check on your progress."

His laughter made my blood curdle. Bending over my prone form, he yanked my skirts aside and retrieved another length of rope from a pocket, then proceeded to bind my ankles together.

"Just in case." He smiled down at his handiwork. "Go ahead and scream as loud as you want to. Nobody'll hear you out here."

It was true, I thought. We'd walked a long way.

"Sleep well," he chuckled, slamming the cabin door. I heard a bolt slide.

His footsteps faded away in the brush. I lay there immobile for another five minutes, straining to hear. Finally I let myself relax. He really was gone. But now I was in a fine pickle.

Locked in a remote cabin, alone. And it was getting dark. I wriggled my hands and feet, but no luck. They were tied too firmly.

A sigh of frustration escaped my lungs. How totally stupid of me to have gotten myself in this predicament. I should have known better than to take off into the forest. At the very least I should kept an eye behind me to make sure I wasn't being followed.

Now what?!

Leaning to one side, I studied what I was able to see of the cabin in the fading light from the window. Nothing helpful that I could see. No tools or implements of any kind. Just that fragile-looking chair and a bare wood floor. And it was getting cold in here. Not to mention darker by the minute.

A small *tink* sounded overhead, followed by a second *tink*, then a third. Naturally. As if I needed any further difficulty, now it was raining. I could only hope the metal roof didn't leak too badly.

Although my feet were tied, I was able to flex my knees. My long skirt made scooting difficult, but after considerable rolling and wriggling I managed to inch myself over to the wall and prop my back against a wooden stud. It still wasn't exactly comfortable. My shoulders ached from having my hands tied behind me so long, and my fingers were going numb.

I bent forward slightly, hoping for a more comfortable position on my spine, then leaned back again.

"Ouch!" I jerked back. I'd pricked a finger on something behind me.

Carefully, I arched my torso slightly, feeling for the object again.

There it was. The protruding point of nail, coming through the outer wall. It wasn't much, but it was something.

Contorting my upper body, I began to work the ropes around my wrists against the sharp edge. Minutes passed. The pounding of rain on the roof grew steadily, then faded.

Eventually I felt one strand of the rope give way. Then another. Suddenly the tension around my wrists was gone. My hands were free!

I rubbed briskly at my aching hands and wrists, then quickly untied my feet.

I tugged at the cabin door, but as expected, it didn't budge. Easing open the small window in the back wall, I stuck my head out. The rain had let up, but daylight had nearly vanished. Still, with the help of the last fading glow in the sky I was able to make out the ground below, sloping steeply away from the cabin. It would be a long drop to the grassy hillside below – one Sylvester Sullivan probably never imagined I would try, even if I did manage to get free.

Sylvester Sullivan didn't know me.

Pulling my head back inside, I grabbed the rickety-looking chair, praying it would hold my weight, and climbed up. Lifting one leg, I straddled the opening, then fed my lower body through first, cussing softly as my heavy skirts snagged and caught on the rough wooden sill. Hurriedly, I ripped the fabric free. Soon my chest was balanced across the windowsill, feet scrabbling against the outside wall. Bit by bit I inched downward until I was hanging by my arms, fingers clutching the narrow sill.

"One, two, three –" I counted to myself, then kicked away from the building and released my hold.

"Oof!" My feet slammed hard into the sloping ground. Tucking into a ball, I let myself collapse and roll.

When I finally came to a stop, the adrenalin jolt had my heart beating double-time. My legs ached, and my wrists and ankles stung from rope-burn. But I was free!

Where to now? I glanced around, unsure whether to risk retracing my steps on the same path Sullivan had used. He'd said he would return to check on me tomorrow. But what if he changed his mind and decided to come back this evening?

Sucking in a breath, I decided I really had no choice. The only way back was the way we had come. I had to risk it.

I needed to get back to the cabin. To Lucas. Much though I was still angry at his deception, Lucas still felt like safety.

I pushed myself up the slope and reached the front of the cabin just as the rising moon began peeking through scattered clouds overhead. It gave just light enough to find the path. Moving slowly and stopping every so often to carefully scan the woods ahead, I followed it back the way I knew we had come. Sullivan, I figured, would bring a lantern if he did try to return.

A fresh band of rain blew in after I'd walked about an hour. Soon my hair and dress were drenched, but I plodded on. Visibility was rotten, forcing me to walk extremely slowly to be sure I kept to the path. But every so often the moon emerged through a hole in the clouds, allowing a clear view of my surroundings and the comfort of knowing I was headed in the right direction.

By the time I made it back to the main road at the edge of the village the storm had intensified. Jagged bursts of lightning alternated with rolling peals of thunder. Ignoring my aching legs I picked up my pace, hoping against hope Sullivan wouldn't find me before I made it back to Lucas' cabin.

I passed a small house on my right, then another on my left, lantern-light from their front windows piercing the darkness. Pretty soon the tall, hulking shape of the inn appeared on my left, with more light streaming onto the roadway from its windows and faint strains of music coming from inside.

Lights were blazing in an upper guest room, too, with shapes of a man and a woman silhouetted against the window. Plowing through the rain and mud, my attention was focused on getting home to Lucas. So, head down, I nearly missed the little drama unfolding in the window. But then I noticed the man's arms pulling the woman into a tight embrace, their bodies molded together in the window. And as my eyes lingered on the romantic couple, I suddenly realized their silhouettes were familiar.

That slight, hunched man was Sullivan. And the lithe woman with the upswept hair in his arms? Amanda.

I was nearly running now, sloshing through the mud puddles, eager to reach the cabin. Sullivan, thank heavens, was otherwise engaged right now. So I could breathe a tad easier knowing he wouldn't be out looking for me.

That was the first piece of good news. And my lips tugged up into a huge grin as I finally put two and two together in the best news of all.

Lucas had been right! Amanda *hadn't* come back for him. She'd claimed Sullivan was her *witness*? Not exactly. Well, yes, but not in the sense she'd pretended.

Sullivan and Amanda were a pair, a couple - and both simply after more gold from Lucas. The two of them had plotted to wring even more money from Lucas with Amanda's breach-of-promise suit. They probably knew his wealthy brother would bankroll a settlement.

The urge to kick myself was back, stronger than ever. I owed Lucas a huge apology. Why had I been so ready to leap to the conclusion he'd deceived me?

Probably because the way I felt about him was - scary. I had to admit that. It was frightening to *need* someone in my life. Especially when I didn't know how long I had with him. And right now, tonight, that prospect seemed shorter than ever.

At long last, Lucas' cabin came into view. I burst through the front door without knocking.

Lucas was seated at the table when I rushed in. He rose from his chair, a look of alarm on his face. A split second later, his arms were wrapped around me.

"Where have you been?" Holding me by my shoulders he stood back, taking in my soggy, disheveled clothes. One finger gently pushed a wet lock of hair from my forehead. "What happened?"

I let him lead me to a chair and wrap me in a blanket, but then I couldn't hold back the rush of words. Quickly, I summarized everything that had occurred – from being kidnapped by Sullivan to escaping through the window of the shack and spotting Sullivan and Amanda in each other's arms as I walked home.

"I owe you a terrible apology for leaping to conclusions about Amanda and what you felt for her," I concluded, when my story finally wound down. "You didn't deserve that."

He tried to shush me, settling a warm hand on my cheek. I reached for both his hands, drawing them into mine.

"No, let me finish. I have one more thing I need to say, and this might be my last chance to say it. I love you, Lucas Russell. You're a good man, a kind man, a hard-working man. And I wish more than anything I could stay right here with you. Because in so many ways, this is where I feel I belong. With you."

His eyes grew moist. "You just made me the happiest man in the world, you know that? And the saddest, at the same time. I thought you were pulling away from me because you didn't care. Not like I care about you. I think I've loved you since the moment I first set eyes on you."

He gazed deep in my eyes. "But I also love you enough that I'm willing to let you go. I know you have to get back to your sister. And if that's where you need to be, believe me, I understand."

A tear slid down my cheek as he pulled me into a tight embrace. I could feel his heart beating against my chest, strong and regular, and knew he was probably feeling my heartbeat, too. This is where I wanted to stay, with every fiber of my being. But my duty to my sister came first.

I lifted my head. There was no more time for talk. Somehow, Lucas already knew what I was going to ask next.

"You want to try again right now, tonight, don't you."

I nodded, brushing a tear away in frustration. I didn't want to cry. Not now. There'd be plenty of time for that later.

"It's still a day or two early. So the moon isn't *quite* full yet. But it's almost there. And so's the Solstice. Most of all, we've got a good storm raging right now, with lightning just like we were waiting for." I studied his eyes. "Once Sullivan goes back to the cabin tomorrow morning and finds me gone, he'll come looking for me. And the first place he'd come is right here. I'm not even sure it will work, making the time-leap tonight. But this feels like the chance I'd been waiting for. I have to take it. And I need your help."

His fingers gripped mine. "You know I'll do anything I can to help. But you also know I'm not planning to come with you?"

I nodded. His place was here. Just as mine was with my sister.

Lucas grabbed his hat from its peg and turned to me. "Alright. Hurry up and get some dry clothes on. I think we've got the mechanics figured out as well as we can. If a good burst of St. Elmo's fire lights up the ship, I think all you need to do is hold onto that pendant and touch the metal railing. And as long as I'm standing clear and not touching that railing or you, I'm pretty sure you'll be the only one making the trip."

Quickly I did as he'd suggested, peeling off my wet clothes while he politely turned his back. It felt both strange and wonderful to throw on the clothes I'd been wearing when I first arrived.

"Ready."

Lucas turned and stepped closer. One finger lightly brushed my cheek. "Are you sure?"

I nodded. "I'm sure."

His mouth was a firm, thin line. This time it was me who pulled him into a hug. He hugged me back with a fierce desperation, then held me at arms' length.

His smile was infinitely kind, and infinitely sad at the same time.

"All right then. Time's a-wasting. Let's go."

Chapter 12
RACHEL

I clenched Lucas' hand as we sloshed our way to the pier where the *Meteor* was moored.

Who knew that asphalt was one of the true wonders of the world?! I certainly missed it right now, as we navigated a road that was more a giant mud puddle than a thoroughfare.

Once on board the ship I waited under the canopy as Lucas went below to fire up the boiler. Off to my right the storm was churning the surface of the lake into whitecaps. Turning back to the shore I took one last look, trying to sear the details into my brain.

I'd made so many happy memories here. All of them involving Lucas.

Pivoting again to stare out across the choppy waves, I burrowed deeper the oilcloth slicker Lucas had insisted I wear, tugging the hood tighter over my head to ward off the chill wind.

The crystal necklace seemed to be growing warmer against my chest. Soon its teardrop shape was burning my skin. Lowering the hood, I pulled the necklace off. The crystal throbbed slowly as I held it up, pulsing with an inner glow. Luckily exposure to the air seemed to dissipate some of the heat; the pendant was warm in my fingers but not too hot to handle.

Jamming the necklace into a pocket, I leaned against the railing. The moon's giant orb was playing hide-and-seek, peeking out intermittently from the clouds, then darting back again. The moon hadn't *quite* reached full, and the summer solstice was two weeks away. But they were close. And given how the necklace was reacting, perhaps tonight would be close enough!

I was thrilled to think I might be back with Serena again soon, if everything went according to plan. But at the same time a painful weight settled in my chest. I'd be losing touch with Lucas forever.

Despite the wooden canopy overhead, the metal deck beneath my feet was slick from blown-in rain and spray. To my left, a thick, round smudge of dirt marred the deck's otherwise-spotless surface. Picking up my feet, I inspected my soles for mud. Happily, it wasn't me who'd tracked the dirt aboard. Perhaps it was from Lucas's boots.

The lightning flashes seemed to pick up their tempo as the ship's engine rumbled to life, giant bursts of light flooding the sky in quick succession. Moments later, Lucas was back at my elbow.

There hadn't been time to loosen the Meteor's lines, so the ship remained firmly secured to the wooden dock. But metal objects on board were already lighting up. A hazy green halo had formed around the ship's bell, and the railing around the deck glittered with a faint, phosphorescent glow. It wasn't just the ship being affected by the strange energy, either. To my right, the surface of the lake was dotted with orbs of iridescent light. Even Lucas himself sported a glowing haze around his shoulders.

It was happening! The metal ship was attracting the storm's intense energy!

I reached for Lucas' hand. A shock rippled through my fingers as we touched, making me recoil. He chuckled.

Pointing to the green glow enveloping the bell, he lifted an eyebrow. "Are you ready? Looks like now's the time."

I swallowed. The moment I'd been waiting for had finally arrived.

"As ready as I'm going to be."

This was it, then. This was good-bye. Stretching up on tiptoe, I kissed him gingerly on the cheek. Happily, that prompted no further sparks between us – of the electrical kind, anyway.

Wrapping one arm about my shoulder, Lucas pulled me in closer. I felt his lips press my hair. Finally he released me and stepped back, his mouth a thin, hard line.

I knew what came next. Slowly, surprised at my own hesitation, I pulled the necklace from my pocket. The crystal had grown even brighter yet. Once again it was hot enough to nearly burn my fingers. Was it just my imagination, or did its inner light glow and ebb with the pulsing and ebbing of the moon? A heartbeat in the sky; an echoing beat between my fingers, they seemed to throb in unison.

Holding the pendant aloft on its silver chain, I slowly raised it to the heavens. Its inner light grew brighter, stronger. All I needed to do now, if our theory was correct, was touch something metal on the ship, and the next lighting flash should transport me home again. To 2023. To Serena.

Pressing my lips together for courage, I stretched out my fingers toward the ship's metal bell. . . .

Lucas grabbed my hand mid-air. "Hold up. I can't let you do this by yourself. Who knows what you'll be walking into on the other end. I need to make sure you're safe."

My brown eyes searched his gentle blue ones. He wasn't saying he'd come with me. Not for good, anyway. He just didn't want me to make this time leap alone. And truth be told, I didn't *want* to go alone.

Trouble was, there were no guarantees with this time-travel business. Yes, he'd made a round-trip once before. But he'd be taking a huge chance. It might not work in reverse a second time.

It was a chance he seemed to want to take, though. And purely selfishly, I wanted it too. It would mean a little more time together.

I nodded. I wasn't quite ready to let him go.

My left hand still twined with his, I raised the crystal toward the sky again with my right. Lucas gave my fingers a soft squeeze and smiled.

Slowly, he stretched out his free hand toward the metal bell. And. . . . A sudden shock flew through me when he touched it.

I was tumbling and falling, my stomach lurching, wrapped in a kaleidoscope of color. A blazing distortion of lights and sound assailed my senses. I squeezed my eyes tight against the onslaught of stimuli.

And then, with a soft thump, my boots hit a hard, a wooden surface. My eyes flew open.

Lucas and I were still side by side; still holding hands. But all evidence of the *Meteor* was gone.

Now, instead of the ship's metal deck, we found ourselves on a long wooden pier – so *very* long I could barely see its ends disappearing in the darkness. Not far away, a handful of empty wooden planters were getting beaten by the driving rain.

It was still pitch dark. Still nighttime. Just as before, huge storm clouds lingered overhead, jagged flashes of lightning bursting from them like fireworks. Rain pelted the shoulders of my oilskin slicker.

Despite the lashing wind and rain, we weren't the only ones at the dock; small clumps of people gathered by the railing, gazing out at the white-capped waves and laughing as if enjoying the storm. Instead of the nearly-empty shoreline I'd grown used to in Lucas' time, dozens of small boats bobbed and heaved in the waves. The wooden fingers of other docks stretched as far as I could see along the water's edge.

To my left, a pair of moving headlights pierced the gloom. A parking lot at the shore-end of the dock, apparently. Squinting, I made out two more cars in the lot, headlights off, windshield wipers going full tilt in the driving rain as they waited.

Was I really back? Yes, obviously modern times, but was it the right *year*? Hastily, I scanned the storm-watchers around me. Bright yellow rain slickers. Sneakers with a signature white swoosh. Women in above-the-knee skirts beneath their umbrellas. A mid-twenties gent with hair swept up in a man-bun snapping pictures of the waves with his iPhone.

I resisted the urge to pump a fist in the air. I still wasn't one hundred percent positive, but – *yes.* It certainly looked as if I'd made it back to 2023!

Beneath the oilcloth slicker I had on my "traveling clothes" – the same jeans and blouse and shoes I'd worn when I first made the unexpected time leap. So nothing about how I was dressed would draw attention like it would have if I'd been wearing one of Charity's long skirts. Luckily, no one seemed to notice our old-fashioned oilcloth slickers as Lucas and I strode casually toward the shore-end of the dock.

Out of the corner of my eye I noticed a lone form separate itself from a clump of looky-loos by the railing and dart ahead of us into the shadows of the parking lot. Something about the shape seemed vaguely familiar. But in the darkness I couldn't get a good look.

As we reached the shore and began making our way through the parking lot, my excitement rose. Soon I would see my sister again!

Lucas took my hand and tried to tuck it in the crook of his arm, but I pulled free and with a smile, simply held his hand instead. I'd have to explain later about why that would draw less attention. He glanced at me quizzically, but kept walking.

Soon, his head was craning this way and that. "I can't believe how crowded it is! And look at all the trees!"

That made me smile. Leave it to Lucas to notice the trees.

For once, I saw the modern world through his eyes. And how very strange it was. Boxy metal vehicles careening about on an ultra-flat roadway, with no draft animals pulling them. Headlights creating pools of light as bright as day. Buildings crammed side-by-side, taller than the tallest trees, where only forest and meadow used to stand.

I didn't want to make Lucas uncomfortable by staring, but risked a quick sideways glance at his face as I steered us through the rain toward my apartment, half a mile away. Slack-jawed, he was soaking in one marvel after another. Concrete sidewalks. LED streetlamps. Business after business, house after house, road after road. He seemed disoriented. Unhappily so, I thought.

The closer we got to my apartment, the more my heart both lifted and twisted. Would Serena be there to greet me? Would she be okay?

Before I knew it, we were climbing the terrazzo steps to my second-floor apartment. A light in the window confirmed somebody was home.

I fidgeted at the front door. Should I knock, or simply walk in? How much time had elapsed here, since I'd left? I had no way of knowing. I settled for knocking, just in case.

Lucas was a reassuring warmth beside me as I lifted my hand. A comforting presence. One eyebrow lifted, silently asking whether I was alright.

With a faint answering smile, I rapped on the door.

Three seconds later Serena was in my arms and I was in hers, tears mingling as we hugged each other tight. And soon we were all seated around my living room, laughing, talking, joking, exchanging high-fives. Well, Serena and I were laughing and joking. Lucas was silently studying the room, a stunned expression on his face.

Right. I could only imagine what he must think of the colorful images on the flat-screen TV. The reclining furniture. The electric lights. The appliances visible in the kitchen beyond the open counter. There was so much I needed to try to explain.

And so much I needed to explain to Serena, too.

Amazingly, it turned out that almost no time at all had passed from her perspective while I'd been gone. She'd been home as usual, waiting for me to return from my evening catering shift, surprised by how late it had gotten. Then surprised by my unexpected knock.

In rapid-fire fashion, I summarized all that had gone on. Well, *most* of it. I decided to leave out those wonderful kisses.

Serena glanced at Lucas repeatedly as I talked. I could see her taking in his muscular forearms and oddly long hair. His cropped-collar shirt and vintage boots. The old-fashioned oilskin slickers we'd hung on pegs beside the door. If what I was telling her seemed unbelievably strange, Lucas himself was Exhibit A, confirming everything was true.

When I reached the end of my narrative I pulled the necklace from my pocket to show it to her. The crystal still emitted a clear, faint light, but its aura now was *so* faint, *so* indistinct, it hardly seemed to be glowing at all.

Serena not only listened thoughtfully, she quickly accepted it all. The only thing that seemed surprising to her was the way I kept reaching over to hug her again and again. I couldn't help myself. It was just so wonderful to be together again, after (for me, at least) four months apart.

For her, however, there'd been no interruption at all; the only break in routine was that I'd brought a stranger home with me.

I hugged Serena one more time. I was thrilled she hadn't worried, and equally thrilled she hadn't managed to manufacture any fresh trouble while I was gone. Glancing over her shoulder, I caught the solemn expression on Lucas' face.

He stood, paced to the front window and stared out at the storm still raging outside. Then he turned back to face me.

"I'd best be going," he said, his voice tight. "I promised to help you get safely home. Now if I'm to get back to my own time, I need to leave while I can."

"The storm." I nodded, releasing Serena. That ache I'd felt earlier in my chest suddenly intensified.

"The storm, and the full moon, and the solstice close," he confirmed. "It's not that those couldn't all happen together again someday. But why waste this opportunity."

Serena stood, staring across the room at him, then glancing down at me.

"Why not just stay here? At least a little while longer. The two of you seem – I dunno." She waved a hand, motioning between us. "You just seem like you kind of like each other."

Our faces lit up with a simultaneous grin.

"We do, Sis," I acknowledged. "It's just –"

"I don't *fit* here," Lucas filled in. "I still have business back in my own time to finish. Things to sort out. A new life to build. I don't want to run away from my troubles. And besides, I left Hasty back in my cabin. He would miss me." Lucas was trying to lighten the mood, I knew, but his smile seemed infinitely sad.

Stepping toward me, Lucas grabbed my hands and pulled me to my feet. "You were right all along, Rachel. Thank you for letting me see all this," he said, those blue eyes fixed on mine. "Change is inevitable. I just need to figure out a way to change with it. Something that will help people enjoy the Lake with hotels and fishing and boating."

My heart felt like it was shattering like glass into teensy, tiny pieces. I'd known he only wanted to make sure I arrived safely. But secretly I'd been hoping he would decide to stay.

I wasn't ready to let him go. Yet I had to.

A frown on her pretty face, Serena glanced from one of us to the other.

"I dunno, you guys. This doesn't feel right," she said, shaking of her head. "You guys seem way too – " Another hand-wave encompassed both of us. "Like, *bonded* or something."

I had to laugh. My wise, wonderful sister. Age seventeen going on forty.

Lucas and I were indeed *something*. We just hadn't had time yet to figure out what that something was. 'Bonded' was probably as good a term as any.

"What do *you* want, Sis?" Serena stepped closer, placing a hand on my shoulder. "You keep trying to protect me and see that I'm happy. But what's going to make *you* happy?"

I flinched. I knew the answer, but I wasn't sure it was the right time to share it. Glancing over at Lucas, I sighed.

She'd asked a straight question. My sister deserved a straight answer.

"If things were different – if I only had myself to think about – I'd go back to 1887 in a heartbeat. I always felt like I was born 150 years too late. There's something that feels *right* about being there. It's a fresh, new world, less hustle and bustle. A community I could easily become part of. And there's —" I shifted my gaze to Lucas. "Someone I care about very much there. But I promised to be your guardian, Serena. I gladly took on that responsibility, and that's more important than anything else. It's why I came back."

"Yes, but I don't want to ruin *your* life." Still frowning, Serena plopped back on the sofa. Biting her lower lip, she wrapped her arms around her knees. "Maybe I could just stay here on my own. Wendy's mom could look out for me. I *am* seventeen, you know."

Sinking to the couch beside her I reached out a hand and ruffled her hair. "Yeah. I know you're seventeen, and you're capable as heck. But it wouldn't be fair to ask Wendy's mom to take on that responsibility. Besides, we're sisters. We need to stick together." That earned me a grin. "Separating our worlds would mean I'd never see you again, and that would be awful."

She looked up at me, the enormity of what time-travel meant finally settling in. "If you go back for good, you would, like, be dead already."

I nodded.

An awkward silence filled the room. Lucas finally broke it.

"I should be going." He took a step toward the door.

My heart began to race. I'd never see *him* again, once he left. Not in this lifetime.

I rose to my feet.

Behind me, Serena's voice sounded tiny, tentative. "Did either one of you consider asking me to come back with you?"

I whirled to face her, my eyes widening. "To 1887? Do you have any idea what life would be like for you there? No cell phones, no texting, no Amazon home delivery?"

Her shoulder lifted in casual dismissal.

"Yeah, yeah. I've read all the Louisa May Alcott books and got an A in American history last quarter. I probably don't know it all, but I think I know enough. Some of it will probably suck. But most of it would be really cool." Her eyes sparkled. "I could learn to ride a horse and drive a buggy. And the clothes would definitely be the bomb, *way* cooler than now.

Steampunk, except for real. Leg o' mutton sleeves and tons of lace, yeah!" Rising to her knees on the sofa, she pumped a thumb's up in the air for emphasis.

I glanced at Lucas. Lucas stared back. The truth was, neither of us had ever considered Serena joining us.

It certainly worked for me. But – would it work for Lucas?

He folded his arms across his chest. Not refusing; merely thoughtful. "There's always a chance you *might* be able to come back to this time someday. But you certainly wouldn't be able to count on it," he cautioned.

"And what about Mark?" I threw in. Not that I really wanted to bring up her ne'er-do-well boyfriend. But did Serena understand? She'd be leaving not only everything but *everyone* she knew behind.

Serena burst into sudden tears. "That's actually why I want to go. Ever since we lost Mom and Dad, life hasn't been exactly grand here. I *know* the crowd I've been hanging with is no good for me. Don't you see? This could be a whole new start." She swiveled to face me. "Maybe there was a reason Mom gave that crystal necklace to you. Did you ever think of that?"

Hunh. No, I'd honestly never considered it. Could Mom have known? Maybe Serena was onto something.

And she was right about something else, too. A fresh start might be very, very good for her. Especially in a simpler age.

Slowly, I nodded. "Sounds like it could be a very good thing."

"Are you certain?" Lucas was putting the question to both of us.

Serena nodded emphatically. "It's not just that the clothes, though those are amazing. It would be a great new adventure."

Lucas' gaze shifted to me.

"Count me in!" I grinned.

It was everything I wanted, and everything I hadn't thought was possible. I knew that the Victorian era was where I belonged. With Rachel. With Lucas. And whatever our combined futures might bring.

"Seems like the decision is made, then." A wide smile spread across Lucas' features. "Sounds like the three of us will 'adapt to the times' together."

My eyes widened. Did Lucas mean what I think he meant?

"That's right." He was looking straight at me. "I know I'll have to start over. But I've seen just now how prosperous the lake will become, and that the land will be beautiful again. It's a future I can help build."

Seizing my hands, he pulled me gently against his chest. "I thought I had to wait to tell you how I felt until I had a fortune to offer you. But you've convinced me *you* see a future for us. And it's one I know we can build together. I love you, Rachel. You'd make me the proudest man on earth if you'd come back and be my wife in earnest." Glancing over at Serena he added. "And I hope you'll consent to being my sister-in-law."

My eyes filled with tears. "I'd love that more than anything in the world."

"Me, too!" Serena chimed in happily.

"Well, then. No time to lose."

Together, the three of us hustled back toward the dock, eager to arrive while the lightning was still flashing. Along the way, Lucas and I briefed Serena on the mechanics for the return journey.

We'd take up the same position on the dock as when we arrived. Then we'd all hold hands while I held the crystal pendant toward the sky. We no longer had a metal ship to focus the storm's energy this time. So we'd need to hope for a bolt of lightning striking *close*.

It was a long-shot, for sure. But all three of us were hopeful.

By the time we stepped onto the long, wooden dock the storm was still thundering around us. Jagged flashes of lightning rent the sky every few seconds, and big, heavy drops of rain splattered against our hair and faces. Lucas and I stood, legs braced against the wind, near the two decorative wooden planters where the magic had dropped us a few hours earlier.

Reaching beneath my slicker I wrapped my fingers around the crystal, drawing the necklace over my head. A faint green glow emanated from the pendant, wrapping itself lightly around my fingers. As I looked up, the orb of the moon emerged suddenly from a break in the scudding clouds.

It felt like an omen. A good one, I hoped.

"Time to link hands," Lucas barked. Smiling, I reached my left hand toward Serena.

But before our fingers could join, an all-too familiar figure strode toward us on the dock. Stopping short of the planters he raised an arm. Something metal glinted in his hand.

It was Sullivan. And he had a gun.

"Ah, I was hoping one of you would come back to the dock tonight," he smirked. "It was a journey I hadn't expected. But now I know for certain that it works."

Moving closer to the planters, he waved the muzzle at me.

"You see, I figured you and Russell would try to make a run for the future together. I found a nice, quiet spot aboard the *Meteor* under a lifeboat where I could watch. I saw you lift that necklace – one piece of the puzzle you cleverly failed to tell me about. It all worked perfectly, didn't it? The storm, the full moon, that fancy necklace. But what I hadn't counted on was that when you opened the portal to the future, I got swept along, too."

I nodded to myself. He'd apparently been close enough that the metal hull linked us.

A satisfied smile wreathed his face. "I hadn't counted on enjoying a ride to the future so soon. But it turned out perfectly. I know exactly how the combination works. So all I need from you now is that necklace. And I do believe you're going to give it to me."

He raised the barrel of the gun, pointing it directly at my chest.

"No!" Serena cried, lunging for Sullivan.

He stepped back behind the planter, the barrel of the gun swinging fast in her direction.

"Wait!" I held the necklace aloft as Lucas grabbed Serena's arm to pull her back. Slowly, the barrel of the gun steadied, then swung back to me again.

My mind raced. No way was I going to simply hand the crystal necklace over to Sullivan. Giving him a key to the time portal was unthinkable. He could wreak all sorts of havoc by changing history. Plus he'd undoubtedly shoot all three of us as soon as he had it.

I glanced up, then down at the planters by my feet. And suddenly I had a plan. It was a huge risk, but I had to try.

The sky was still alive with thunder and lightning.

"Here, catch!" I said, tossing the necklace lightly to Lucas. He caught it in one hand.

Had Lucas understood my unspoken message? *Just buy us some time. . . and if a flash of lightning happens to come along at the right second. . .*

Grinning, Lucas swung the pendant high overhead as if he contemplated throwing it into the lake's churning waters. "Is this what you want, Sullivan?" he taunted.

Sullivan's face contorted in anger.

Behind us, a flash of lightning hit the water, followed almost instantly by a clap of thunder. That one was *close.*

The pendant in Lucas' hand had swelled to a brilliant green orb, beating like a living heart. *Pulsing, pulsing. . .*

His face red, Sullivan took a step closer to the planter by my feet, the barrel of his gun pointed straight at me.

"Hand it over *now*, Russell. No more games. You know I won't hesitate to use this."

The gun may have been pointed at me, but Sullivan's focus was on Lucas and the pendant. Quickly I stooped and grabbed a handful of dirt from the planter and threw it in Sullivan's eyes. He screamed and dropped the gun, rubbing at his eyes with both hands.

It was the chance Lucas and I had been waiting for. I seized Serena's forearm just as Lucas reached out a hand and grabbed mine. Extending his other arm as high as he could, Lucas held the pulsing crystal toward the sky – at exactly the moment another jagged arrow of lightning appeared.

Timing was everything. And ours proved impeccable.

An instant later my heels clanged hard against the metal deck of the *Meteor*. And there we were, all three of us. Laughing, we exchanged jubilant high-fives.

Lucas, Serena, and I had made it back in 1887. Together.

And best of all, we'd left Sullivan firmly stuck in the future, where he couldn't bother us again.

Epilogue

How much had changed since the Snow Moon first whisked me here, I found myself thinking that following June.

Had it really only been a year ago? Well, more than a year, really, since I arrived with the Snow Moon last February.

It had been a full year. A good year. A year that turned so many hopes into reality.

In place of the winter's snow and fall's crisp autumn colors, June flowers now dotted the meadow again. Serena was ready to graduate from high school.

It hadn't been as easy a transition for her as she'd expected. Turns out that Victorian schoolwork was significantly harder than she was used to – and there was no internet to help with homework.

But I was immensely proud of her. She'd made it work. And I'd been *thrilled* she'd quickly found a wide group of friends among a much better crowd.

Before my eyes, she had turned into quite the accomplished young lady. She could sew, she could sing, and she'd even developed a surprising fondness for math. Her fiery temper hadn't changed one whit, however. She definitely still had her own mind—and freely expressed it.

We'd been talking the last few weeks about what she might do now that she was eighteen and all grown up. Well, in her own eyes, anyway. These staid Victorians believed you had to be twenty-one to officially be considered an adult.

Thankfully, women here in the West enjoyed a tiny bit more latitude. Women still couldn't vote yet (something that seriously chapped my hide, even though I knew it would eventually change). But young ladies often left home to become schoolteachers, or ladies' companions, or governesses. Some opened their own dress-making or millinery shops. Others, of course, married much younger than eighteen. I shuddered inwardly at that thought, grateful Serena hadn't gone down that road.

There'd been some cute boys in her class. Thankfully, Serena still seemed immune to any matrimonial ideas.

I settled at my desk by the window, determined to capture a few menu ideas that had been floating in my head. Lucas and I had worked hard to brainstorm business ideas to tap Lake Tahoe's tourist appeal, and he'd recently broken ground on a small luxury hotel we hoped to open this summer. "The name 'Tahoe Tavern' has a fine ring to it," he'd suggested just yesterday. I'd only smiled, biting my lip so I didn't tell him how famous the name would become.

At my suggestion, he'd converted the *Meteor* into a stylish passenger steamer to carry visitors on fishing trips around the lake. That enterprise, too, should do well in the coming summer, especially with the rail line now connecting North Shore with Truckee.

Lucas had successfully sold off a piece of his timber land last fall, and had managed to persuade Sullivan's bank partners that a performing loan looked a whole lot better in their portfolio than a foreclosure. With that cash in hand plus the business plan I'd helped him develop, Lucas got them to extend the deadline on his loan. With any luck, he'd soon be paying off the balance.

As for me, I'd been excitedly dreaming up menus and designing the new hotel's kitchen. It certainly was a different 'dream come true' than I ever imagined, but a perfect fit for a someone like me who truly loved to cook! Together, Lucas and I were confident our new enterprises would be a success.

My thoughts were suddenly interrupted as Lucas breezed through the front door, Hasty at his heels. Looping an arm about my waist he planted a sudden kiss on my cheek.

"You know what I'm grateful for right now?" he whispered in my ear.

"My cooking?"

He laughed. "No. Well, yes, but that's not what I had in mind. I happened to run into Amanda at the grocer's in town earlier today, and was thinking how grateful I am to have escaped that woman's clutches. That is one unhappy woman!"

Thanks to Sullivan's mysterious disappearance, Amanda had been forced to drop her breach of promise suit, since she no longer had a witness. Rumors of her dalliance with Sullivan had spread through the community, and most of the town wanted nothing to do with her. She was one unhappy woman, indeed.

I turned and gave Lucas a quick kiss in return. "And I'm one very *happy* wife!" We'd snuck away to Sacramento last fall and quietly tied the knot for real. I truly couldn't imagine being happier.

Lucas took my hands in his. "And I'm ever so grateful you convinced me to keep trying. To not wallow in failure when my original plan wasn't working."Slowly, I traced a finger over the wide gold wedding band he wore on his left hand – a clone of the smaller one on mine.

"You weren't a failure, Lucas. Things change. That's the nature of life. We just have to be willing to change with them."

Dipping his head to steal another kiss, he softly threaded his fingers through mine. Our hands a perfect fit, like everything else about us.

"With you here at my side, I'm confident we'll continue to do just that," he grinned.

I touched his face. "But come to think of it, I owe you an apology."

"For what?"

"For not trusting you, when you told me your relationship with Amanda was already over." I'd never grow tired of staring into those amazing blue eyes. "Though I really do need to ask why you've kept her love letters."

His brows contracted. "Amanda's love letters? What on earth are you talking about?"

Suddenly he burst out in a hearty laugh. "You mean that packet of letters I kept on the bedside table? The ones you made me put in the back of the cupboard? *Those* letters?"

I nodded, puzzled.

"Those were from my mother! She wrote me many times before she passed away. As you can imagine, I couldn't bear to throw them out."

Both of us dissolved in laughter. It was a perfect object lesson about not leaping to conclusions. All this time I'd assumed those letters were from Amanda!

We chuckled even harder when a neighbor stopped by later that afternoon to inform us he'd spotted Amanda boarding the stage, a raft of trunks in tow. Hank Monk was no longer the one in command of the reins, of course. But his replacement had quietly whispered that he planned to ensure that Amanda enjoyed a ride "every bit as speedy as Horace Greeley's" to her next destination.

Lucas and I were wrapping our arms around each other, preparing to share yet another sweet kiss, when Serena burst into the room, eyes dancing with excitement.

"Look at this!" she cried, waving a newspaper under our noses. "I've been wondering what I would do when I graduate. Doesn't this sound like a perfect fit for me?"

Lucas grabbed the paper from her hand.

"Wait. The Jules Trent? Brash, arrogant and moneyed? Lost his wife a few years ago, and said to be the handsomest man in Bodie?"

"Handsome? Better yet," Serena smirked. "Sounds like a job made in heaven!"

Snatching the newspaper from Lucas, I quickly scanned the ad where Serena pointed.

"Governess wanted for two orphaned girls," it read. "Must be docile and refined. Steady position, $30 per month. Apply in person. J. Trent Hotel, Bodie."

A brash, arrogant, *handsome* widower was looking for a governess for his young daughters? And hard-headed, opinionated Serena, trying to pretend she was docile and refined? It hardly sounded like a perfect fit to me.

It was, in fact, the worst match imaginable. *And that, dear Reader, is the beginning of yet another fine tale!*

<u>*Historical Notes*</u>: Thank you for reading *Snow Moon*! The main characters and events in this book were pure fiction, of course. But many of the historical details were real.

The "Big Bonanza" on the Comstock was struck in 1873, eventually producing over $100 million. Its peak silver mining years were 1876 to 1878. But as the book suggests, by 1879 the lodes were beginning to play out. Ore production declined sharply – prompting a similar drop in demand for timber. Subsequent events didn't help, including water that flooded the lower levels of the Comstock in 1882. At Glenbrook, the sawmill owned by Carson and Tahoe Lumber & Fluming Co. burned in October 1887, a significant $15,000 loss.

There really was a *Glenbrook House*, erected about 1863 by Goff and Morrill as the first hotel in the vicinity of Glenbrook. It sat half a mile from the shore of Lake Tahoe, and served travelers on the Lake Bigler Toll Road that ran up Kings Canyon. A similar-sounding but completely different *Glenbrook Inn* was launched in 1906 by the Bliss family. This was actually a combination of three remodeled buildings. Capt. Pray's general store, originally built on a pier, was moved north of Lake Shore House to become the main building of the Inn (including lobby, dining room, office, kitchen, and an upstairs dance hall). The nearby Lake Shore House provided additional guest rooms. And the old Jellerson Hotel was moved north of the general store to offer even more rooms. Nearby sat the large Bliss house, and new cottages were eventually built as part of the complex.

The Glenbrook community at the time our fictional characters were there would have been quite small - there were just 335 souls in 1880, dropping to 223 by 1890. But festive parties really did take place at Rowlands' Customs House, a saloon built out over the water on a pier on the South Shore. Sophronia Rowland would still have been running the business after losing her husband, Thomas Rowland, in 1883. Rowland's hotel would collapse in the winter of 1889-90.

There really was a *Meteor,* a 75-foot long "iron steamer" acquired in 1886 by Bliss's Carson and Tahoe Lumber & Fluming Co. (not Lucas). There also really was a Capt. A.J. Todman who owned the *Tod Goodwin* pleasure steamer in 1887 and had a large fish hatchery which planted 1.5 million trout in the waters of Tahoe that year. There also really was a George W. Chubbock who ran a logging camp at Rowlands described by a contemporary newspaper as "in full blast" in April 1887.

Sadly, much of the virgin timber near Tahoe had been logged off by 1893. D.L. Bliss heeded the concerns of visitors about the eradication of Tahoe's old-growth lumber and ordered his loggers on his timber tracts to spare any trees less than 15 inches in diameter to encourage regrowth. In real life, Bliss clearly recognized Lake Tahoe's tourist appeal; he purchased a stylish passenger steamer; linked the North Shore by rail to Truckee; and built a luxury hotel, the Tahoe Tavern, which opened in 1902. I've used fictional license to attribute some of those plans to Lucas, moving them earlier than they really happened.

Most amazing of all, an electrical storm similar to the one described in this book *did* happen on Lake Tahoe, and actually did "light up" the iron steamship *Meteor* in 1887 with "sheets of lurid light"! The event was described in vivid detail in the *Genoa Weekly Courier* of May 27, 1887, including a "phosphorescent haze cover[ing] the whole surface of the water" and "blotches of phosphorescent light" dotting the steamship. One of these glowing orbs reportedly: "attached itself to Capt. Pomin, and when Fred Bodine, the engineer, playfully touched it with his finger he received a shock, accompanied by a loud report, that caused him to recoil in amazement." So it was great fun to incorporate that real-life story into this book!

Thanks So Much for Reading!

This isn't really the end! There's more time-transcending travel and unexpected love in the rest of the **Blue Moon** series!

Check out ***Solstice Moon,*** which shares the time-traveling story of Rachel's friend, Charity (who made a cameo appearance in this book). As the tale begins, Charity is working as a docent at the famous Danforth mansion in Carson Valley when a splash of solstice magic pitches her back to 1885 – and face-to-face with the home's original owner, who thinks she's seeking a job! Both Charity and Josiah are dead-set against romance and determined to fight the attraction that blossoms between them. But will love change their future? Visit Amazon.com to learn more about ***Solstice Moon***!

In the second book of the series, ***Harvest Moon***, Jake's search for hidden treasure takes a wild turn when he finds himself cast back in time to Virginia City in 1886. There he stumbles across pretty Eliza, on the run from a ruthless and dishonest uncle. Find ***Harvest Moon*** at Amazon!

Eager to know when the *next* time-travel tale in the **Blue Moon Series** is released? Join my VIP Readers list at AbbyRiceAuthor.com, and I'll be sure you're among the first to hear the news!

And if you're hungering for a full-length historical/adventure romance (plucky heroine, grumbly sea captain, fake marriage, plus the Welsh gift of second sight!), check out ***The Captain's Kidnapped Bride*** on Amazon!

About the Author:

Abby Rice was treated to plenty of tall tales of the courtroom variety while working as a criminal prosecutor. Now she's happily spinning fun tales of her own as a writer. Most days you can find her inhaling coffee, nose-deep in an old newspaper, or wrangling strong-willed characters determined to plunge off on some tangent of their own. In between books, she's probably dreaming up her own next adventure (anywhere with palm trees!)

Let's Stay Connected!

Like to stay in touch? Join Abby's *free* monthly email sharing her author world, bits of crazy-wonderful Victoriana, occasional short stories, and inside-glimpses from Abby's latest romance-in-progress. Subscribe at AbbyRiceAuthor.com.

Made in United States
Troutdale, OR
10/24/2024